"You didn't think you were *staying* here?"

Will nodded. "For baby lessons. You said you'd teach me how to take care of her."

"Not tonight, I didn't."

"Daisy, who else can I ask? Just about everybody in town thinks I'm nothing more than a rodeo stud."

She couldn't disagree with that. "A rodeo stud who now has a baby to care for. Go home and get some rest. Besides, everyone will see your car parked outside."

"It's parked at the gas station. It'll look like it needs work."

"I should have minded my own business."

Will crossed the space between them in one stride. He smiled into her eyes. "Now, honey, what kind of fun is that?"

"Don't 'honey' me." Daisy studied the man determined to spend the night in her house. He was handsome, but he was a little crazy, too. The charming cowboys always were.

Dear Reader,

As you know by now, I love writing about cowboys and babies. There's something special about a tough Western hero learning to deal with a helpless child—especially if there's a woman looking over his shoulder telling him he's going about things all the wrong way! In *Billy and the Kid*, the baby never stops crying and Daisy, an outspoken waitress with a heart of gold is appalled that anyone would leave an infant with town bad boy Will Wilson. And Billy? Well, he knows that once again he's in big trouble, but he's not about to let a little baby change his life...too much.

I hope you'll look for my BOOTS & BOOTIES by Request book next month. If you missed the first three BOOTS & BOOTIES stories when they were first published in Temptation, here's another chance to read them.

Thank you, too, for all the wonderful letters. I'm so glad you're enjoying my books!

Sincerely,

Kristine Rolofson

Kristine Rolofson

BILLY AND THE KID

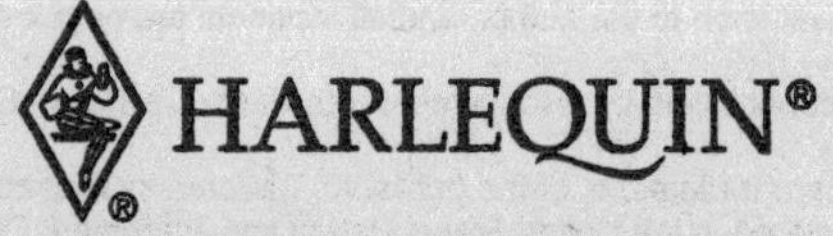

TORONTO • NEW YORK • LONDON
AMSTERDAM • PARIS • SYDNEY • HAMBURG
STOCKHOLM • ATHENS • TOKYO • MILAN • MADRID
PRAGUE • WARSAW • BUDAPEST • AUCKLAND

To Minnie and Martha,
who help in more ways than they will ever know.

ISBN 0-373-25865-8

BILLY AND THE KID

This edition published by arrangement with Harlequin Books S.A.

Visit us at www.romance.net

Printed in U.S.A.

1

IF HE HADN'T been dreaming of spring, he'd have heard the dog barking. At the very least, he'd have opened his eyes. Maybe he would have made it out of bed and onto his feet. Maybe he would have even thought to peer through the holes in the old lace curtain to see who was down below, banging on the front door of the house. As it was, Will woke in time to hear the dog whining over the sound of a rapidly fading truck engine.

Whoever it was would come back, he figured, though anyone who knew him would have opened the door and yelled up the stairs for at least ten minutes. Will wasn't known for "early to bed, early to rise" habits. Once he was asleep there wasn't much any man could do to wake him. But a woman? Will smiled and stretched in his sleeping bag. He always woke when there was a warm and willing woman beside him in bed in the morning. Too bad he couldn't remember the last time anything so pleasurable had happened.

Damn the dog.

"Boze! Shut up!"

Bozeman continued to cry, a high-pitched sound that would have killed a man who had a hangover, so Will was grateful he'd only had that one beer last night while he'd watched television. He shoved his bedding aside, got out of bed and walked over to the open doorway. "Hey, Boze, take it easy, boy."

The dog whined louder, punctuating each whine with a pitiful bark that could only mean one thing: Get your sorry ass down here, Will, and help me.

So Will picked up his jeans and pulled them on before he went downstairs to find out what had gotten him up at the crack of—he glanced at the grandfather clock on the landing—7:59 in the morning. Bozeman, tail wagging, was in the hall to greet him. "So what's your problem?"

The dog turned to the door that faced the front porch.

"All this is because you want to go out?" Will jerked open the door, but Bozeman's white, fluffy body didn't budge. "Go on, and—"

That's when he saw the basket nestled against the step. For a split second he thought he'd left his laundry on the porch. He didn't recognize the faded patchwork quilt, but when he bent down to get a better look he discovered it covered something. "Oh, hell," Will grumbled. "If someone's left pups out here again—"

He stopped the second he pulled the quilt halfway down, for there on the front porch of the Triple T Ranch house lay a tiny, sleeping baby. Bozeman sidled up beside Will to sniff for himself, then he turned tail and ran. Will knelt down and watched the baby's eyelids flutter, as if the little thing was dreaming. Or trying to wake up.

But why was it on his front porch? He knew there was no sense going after that truck, but as he lifted the basket and carried it inside the house, it did occur to him that someone might be playing a joke on him. Wouldn't be the first time, or the last, but this wasn't all that funny. Not yet.

He shoved stacks of papers aside and set the basket in the middle of the round oak table, the cleanest place he could think of. Even though he'd never dealt with an infant before, he knew enough to know they were supposed to hang out in clean places. Nothing on the ranch fit that description, not even its owner, but at least the center of the dining-room table kept the baby in a safe place while Will made a whispered phone call from the kitchen.

Then Will prayed the kid would continue sleeping for as long as it took for Pierce to get the hell out to the Triple T. He made a pot of coffee, put on a shirt he found on the couch, let Bozeman out the back door. The baby slept, completely oblivious to its surroundings, until the deputy sheriff banged on the back door.

"This had better be good," Pierce grumbled, shaking the snow off his hat before he entered the kitchen, Bozeman slipping inside with him. "I didn't even have time to make coffee."

"Keep your voice down." Will poured coffee into two mugs and handed one to his oldest friend. "I've got enough trouble without waking the baby."

"What baby?" He took the coffee and glanced around the cluttered kitchen. "You've got company?"

"You could say that." Will led the way into the dining room. "Check it out," he said, motioning toward the basket. "Someone left it here this morning."

Pierce stepped closer and peered into the baby's face. "Is that what I think it is?"

Will pulled out a chair and sat down as he watched Pierce set his mug on the table. The sheriff lifted the blanket and poked underneath.

"What the hell are you doing? It'll wake up."

"Looking for a note. Shh, there, baby. Old Uncle Pierce just wants to find out who you are."

The baby opened its eyes and started to fuss. Pierce pulled out a plastic bottle filled with milk. "You lucked out," he said. "The baby came with its own breakfast."

"I lucked out? This has nothing to do with me. I think the police should—"

Pierce ignored him. "It's wet under here. Let's hope there are some diapers."

"Diapers?"

"Wait," he said, pulling out a folded piece of paper. He handed it to Will. "No diapers, but this has got your name on it, so I'm going to go out on a limb here and say this has plenty to do with you. Read it."

Will shook his head. "I am not the father of this baby."

"Someone thinks you are."

The topic of conversation waved its tiny fists in the air and let out a howl that had Bozeman heading for the door again. Will tossed the note on the table as if it were a live snake. He looked at the screaming baby and frowned. "Hell, Pierce, what do I do with it?"

"You feed it. Stick this bottle in a pan of hot water for a couple of minutes and then you feed it."

Will took the bottle, but he hesitated. "Shouldn't you be taking it to a hospital or something?"

"One step at a time, Billy my boy," his friend said, reaching into the basket. He scooped the baby into his arms, wadded the small blanket around the baby's bottom and tucked the whole bundle against his uniformed chest. "You want to turn up the heat in here?"

He could do that, no problem. He'd had the furnace replaced last month, so that was one thing in the house that worked. He ran the water until it turned hot, then gingerly put the bottle into the pan. "How long do I do this?"

"A few minutes. Come back here and tell me why you think this kid isn't yours." Pierce pulled out a chair and, with the baby tucked against his chest, made himself comfortable. "You haven't exactly lived a, uh, sheltered life. In fact, your rodeo days are the stuff of legends."

Will wondered how the man could hold a baby and drink coffee at the same time. "I was young then and full of hell," he said, eyeing the note with his name scrawled on it. He'd had enough wild adventures to fill several lifetimes, but he'd always been careful. He didn't want kids and he didn't want AIDs and he sure as hell didn't want any paternity suits. "Just take my word for it."

Pierce took another sip of coffee. "Read."

Will didn't recognize the writing. Girlish loops and blue ink on a piece of lined notebook paper made the letter look as innocent as a note passed in high school. His callused fingers fumbled with the paper, but he finally got it open. "Willie," it began, which was odd. Women who knew him from his rodeo days called him "Billy."

"You going to keep us in suspense or are you going to read it out loud?" Pierce rocked the baby a little and it stopped fussing.

"Are you sure you should be doing that?"

"What?"

"Bouncing it like that. You might hurt it."

"I have two boys, Will, and one more due any day, remember?" Pierce chuckled. "I know what I'm doing. Quit stalling and read."

Will turned back to the paper. He had a feeling he wasn't going to like what was coming. "Willie," he repeated. "I figure this baby belongs to you now. I would've kept her, but she needs a family and I don't—" He swore and held up the paper. "The ink ran and I can't read the rest."

"Convenient."

"I'm serious. Here." He handed Pierce the note. "I think the kid must have peed on it or something."

The sheriff held it to the light. "I think the bottle leaked."

"At least we know she's a girl."

"A girl," Pierce mused, looking down at the baby. "Janie's hoping for a girl this time around. I don't know how she'll feel if it's a third boy."

"You could give her this one," Will offered, sensing an answer to his problem. But even as he said it, he knew that if this kid really was his, she wouldn't be going anywhere. There'd been enough unwanted Wilson kids in this county already.

"Get the bottle, you idiot. Then I'll teach you how to feed your daughter."

"She's not mine. I've done some crazy things in my time, but I've never been that stupid," Will insisted, hurrying into the kitchen to retrieve the milk. He wiped the dripping bottle on his sleeve and peered into the baby's face as if she might give him some clue to her identity. "Do you think she looks like me?"

"Maybe. Hard to tell. Babies usually have blue eyes when they're born, and that light hair of hers could darken. Shake some of that milk on your hand and make sure it's not too hot."

He did as he was told. "What am I supposed to do, Joe?"

His friend considered the question for a long moment while the baby fussed in his arms. "I can take her in to the office and then I'll contact the state people. We can say you found her and called me."

"Which is the truth."

"But—" Joe Pierce held Will's gaze with his own "—she'll end up in a foster home until I can track down her mother."

"*If* you can find her."

"You know how that goes."

"Yeah." He knew, all right.

"Here." Pierce leaned forward and deposited the baby into Will's arms. "Just hold her up a little and give her the bottle. Half of it, then you have to burp her."

The little thing seemed to know what to do. And acted like she hadn't eaten in a week. He looked over toward Pierce. "You don't suppose—"

His best friend since sixth grade waited. And thought. And then his eyes widened. "No. Couldn't be."

Will felt like laughing. "Sure it could. She and my mother were the only people who ever called me Willie, remember?"

Pierce leaned closer to stare into the child's face. Milk dribbled from the corners of her tiny mouth and down her neck, into her yellow terry-cloth sleeper, but neither man noticed. "God, it's been years."

"Sarah's little girl," Will said, his heart lifting in an unfamiliar way as he held the baby against him. "I'll need to buy some stuff."

Pierce nodded. "Yeah. And you should take her into the clinic and make sure she's in good shape."

"You think there's something wrong?"

"No, she looks fine to me, but we don't know where she's been or who she is and—"

The baby screeched when Will took the bottle away. "With that kind of temper, I'm pretty sure I know who she is," he said. "What I don't know is what I'm supposed to do to get her to stop yelling at me."

"Lift her up, put her against your shoulder and pat her back until she burps."

Will did, and the baby hiccuped against his collar. She was warm and soggy and she didn't smell too good, but he didn't care. Will Rogers Wilson knew damn well that this kid wasn't going anywhere.

Not until he found her mother.

"YOU NEED A MAN."

"No one needs a man," Daisy lied, wiping the counter with a damp sponge. She looked at the clock over the door of The Cowman's Café. Only noon, and she had five more hours left until she could start closing up. Even though she closed early, Sundays were endless, especially in the only restaurant in the smallest town in the county. "Trust me, some men are more trouble than they're worth."

"I hope I don't feel that way when I get as old as you," the younger woman said, smoothing her dark red hair behind her ears to reveal a pair of silver earrings the shape of cowboy boots. "You want some gum?"

"No, thanks." Daisy ignored the "old" remark. After all, she felt twice as old as her twenty-eight years and light years older than the teenage waitress who worked for her. It was a wonder she didn't have gray hair and crow's feet instead of blond curls. She fixed herself a cup of herbal tea and hoped she'd have time to drink some of it. Here she'd thought the snow would keep people home, but nothing seemed to prevent the people of Cowman's Corner from having dinner at the café.

"I don't know how you stand it, staying home all the time. Not that there are that many guys around here to go out with," Heather said, popping a piece of gum in her mouth.

"You don't seem to have any shortage of dates." She dunked her tea bag a few times and tossed it in the trash can.

"I meant for you. Everyone's either too young or too old or married or drinks too much or is broke."

"That's a little harsh," Daisy pointed out, but she chuckled anyway. She'd thought the same thing more than a few times in the months since she'd moved to town. Not that the quality of men had anything to do with her life here and now, of course, but it didn't hurt to be polite and go along with a conversation. Especially during a lull in business. She wouldn't mind going out on a date with someone nice. Sometimes, in weak and foolish moments, she even thought about marriage and babies and a cozy little house.

"Maybe you should be nicer to the old ones," the young woman advised. "You don't want to be a waitress all your life, do you?"

"When I'm old I'll put this place up for sale and retire to Hawaii," Daisy declared, sipping her tea. The bell over the door jangled as two snow-covered men entered the room. The man with the sheriff carried a bundle that looked like a baby.

"Oh, wow, it's him." Heather smoothed her hair again. "Who gets him today?"

"Who? Sheriff Pierce?"

Heather shook her head. "Billy the Kid."

An idiotic name for a grown man, Daisy thought. "You can have him."

"Really?" The girl's face lit up.

"Be my guest." The bell jangled, admitting another couple into the room, so Daisy set her tea down and picked up a couple of menus.

"No, I can't." Heather sighed. "Mom and Dad just walked in. Looks like today is your lucky day, because I'll get in big trouble if Billy flirts with me and I look like I'm liking it."

"I'll wait on your parents," Daisy said, happy for any excuse to avoid booth nine. Billy Wilson left the waitresses at the café overly generous tips, but as far as Daisy was concerned, the man was the biggest pain in the rear of them all. That kind of man always was. She reminded herself that she was certainly immune to blue eyes and dark lashes and a fine set of shoulders. She was definitely unaffected by his wicked "come to me, baby" smile and all that lazy charm he poured on every woman within drawling distance.

"Go ahead, wait on Billy," Heather said. "Maybe he'll liven up your afternoon."

Daisy would have laughed, but the girl was right. Billy Wilson did have a way of making a woman feel alive. Physically alive, in a self-conscious way. And getting physical with anyone was the last thing Daisy wanted to think about. Celibacy was dull, but certainly less risky than making another mistake.

She picked up a couple of menus and took her time walking across the room to where the sheriff was hanging up his heavy green coat. Billy was holding a baby, which certainly was a strange sight. The cowboy didn't look as if he was used to carting around an infant. Daisy tried not to stare, but she couldn't help taking a quick peek at the quilt-wrapped bundle as she dropped the menus on the table. The child looked about two months old, a tiny thing with closed eyes and pink cheeks. Pretty and delicate, the baby looked nothing like either man. Still, Daisy tried not to appear too curious. It was none of her business if Billy Wilson laid a baby beside him in the booth.

"Coffee?" she asked, knowing that the lanky sheriff lived on the stuff.

"Thanks."

She turned to Billy. "Coffee for you, too?" He nodded, but there was no accompanying smile. In fact, Daisy thought he looked a little pale. "Our Sunday specials are meat loaf with mashed potatoes and green beans, your choice of pie for dessert, or roast chicken with the same—potatoes, beans and pie."

"Meat loaf," a very subdued cowboy said. "And coffee. Lots of it."

"Sure. Sheriff?"

"I'll have the same. And three hamburgers and fries to take home with me in about half an hour, thanks."

"How's your wife doing?"

"Tired of being pregnant," Joe said. "The doctor told her to stay off her feet for the next couple of weeks, but it's not easy for her."

"Tell her I said hello."

"Sure."

"I'll get your coffee."

"Just a sec." Billy Wilson reached into his jacket pocket and pulled out a baby bottle. "You mind warming her bottle for me?"

"No problem," she said, taking the bottle from his outstretched hand. As she turned away she heard the sheriff say, "See, Will? I told you fatherhood would be easy."

Fatherhood? Daisy resisted the urge to turn around and gape at the two men. Instead she hurried across the room and grabbed a metal milkshake can. Billy, the wildest guy in town, was a father? That poor kid.

She half filled the can with hot water and carefully placed the bottle inside.

"It's his baby, isn't it?" Barlow, the cook, peered through the opening that divided the kitchen from the rest of the café. Heather leaned over and clipped her parents' order to the board.

"I don't think so. Why would he have a baby? He's not the type."

"Hey," the man said, ignoring the order. "Anyone's the type."

"What type?" Daisy asked, placing her slip next to Heather's. "Two meat specials now, three burgs to go later."

Heather lowered her voice. "The type to have a kid. Do you think it's his? I mean, the sheriff hasn't had his baby yet, has he?"

"No. Jane's still pregnant."

"Then whose baby is it?" the cook demanded.

She glanced over her shoulder at the two men, who looked as if they were discussing the fate of the world. "I think it's the cowboy's."

Barlow, an aging hippie who looked as if he'd done his share of drugs in the sixties, shook his head as if he still couldn't believe his ears. "Billy the Kid with a kid. How about that?"

"THERE'S THE ANSWER to my problem," Will said.

"Daisy McGregor?" Pierce rolled his eyes. "I don't think she's exactly the maternal type."

"I'm not talking about Daisy. That woman is as mean as my grandmother's old dog," he muttered, watching her pour coffee into two mugs. "I was thinking of Heather, the young one."

"Thinking of Heather for what?"

"A baby-sitter. I can't take care of a baby and get

that ranch ready to sell at the same time. Hell, I'm still trying to recover from the whole diaper-changing thing."

"Jane would help, but she can't, not with being two weeks away from having the baby. And the Little Critters day-care center doesn't take kids until they're two."

Will watched Daisy fuss with the bottle. That little lady could sure fill out a pair of jeans. "What's Little Critters?"

Pierce shuddered. "If you're determined to keep this baby, you've got a lot to learn. Really, Will, maybe you should think about turning her over to the state, just until you figure out if she's Sarah's or not."

"I'm not giving Sarah's baby to strangers."

"And if she isn't Sarah's? What if someone is trying to saddle you with somebody else's kid? God knows you've known enough women that someone could do this, pass this little girl on to you and then show up demanding child support."

"That's what DNA tests are for, right?" He didn't feel as casual as he let on. His stomach was in knots and he hoped he'd be able to choke down some of Barlow's famous meat loaf. What had seemed like a good idea three hours ago now began to feel downright scary, especially now that the baby was waking up again and making noises. Will couldn't remember when he'd been this scared. Not since he was twelve, anyway. And that was a time he didn't want to spend much time remembering.

"I need someone to take care of this baby until we can find Sarah."

"You can't have Heather out to the ranch. Her father would shoot you."

"Yeah, I guess you're right." He looked over at the baby, who opened her eyes and made a small mewing sound. "But I'm sure going to need help."

"Hire an older, grandmotherly type."

"Are you kidding? Those old gossips would have a hell of a time talking about this baby, wouldn't they? I'm not going to give them the chance."

Daisy delivered the coffee and the bottle. "It's warm. I checked it."

"Thanks."

She stayed by the table and watched as Will unwrapped the baby's quilt. The little girl started to scream and didn't stop until Will had arranged her in his arms and popped the nipple into her mouth.

Daisy slid the coffee cups away from the flailing arm of the baby. "Are you sure you know what you're doing?"

Will frowned into a pair of gorgeous blue eyes. "No. Go away."

"Her head's too low."

Will looked at Pierce, who nodded, so he lifted the child's head a little higher. Daisy leaned over and took some napkins from the dispenser, which gave Will a nice view of the way her breasts filled out her blue T-shirt. "Here," she said, holding the napkins gently against the baby's chin. "She's going to be dripping wet. Do you have other clothes for her?"

"Yeah."

"And more bottles?"

"Yes. Whoa there." He eased the half-empty bottle out of the baby's mouth. The little stinker glared at him and started to scream. "Hey, honey, you've got to burp." He looked at Pierce. "Right?"

"Yeah. Pat. Burp." The sheriff pulled his beeper out of his shirt pocket. "Sorry, Will, but I'm being paged." He stood and grabbed his hat and coat. "Call me and let me know what you decide to do with her. You can call Jane, too, if you have questions."

If he had questions? Will felt the now-familiar panic filling his gut again. "You're not coming back?"

"I'm not sure. Depends on what's going on." He hesitated as he shrugged into his coat and turned to Daisy. "Is it too late to put a hold on those burgers? I don't know when I'll get back."

"I'll have them sent over to your house," Daisy assured him.

"I'll do it," Will said, raising his voice over the screams of the baby. He lowered her into feeding position and stuck the bottle in her mouth.

"You've got enough to do," Pierce told him, with a quick wave of his hand. Then he smiled at Daisy. "Thanks."

The annoying waitress stood at the end of the table as if she'd been roped and tied there until the baby sucked down the remaining milk, spat out the nipple, and screamed even louder than she had before.

Daisy—a ridiculous name for such a humorless woman—cast that blue-eyed gaze in his direction. "Where are they?"

"Where are who?" No way was he going to tell her that he didn't know where this kid's parents were, though right about now he'd have given a fistful of silver belt buckles to find out.

"The clothes and the bottles and the formula and the diapers."

"Oh. In my truck." Sarah's baby had ridden into town snug in her basket on the floor of his truck, though Pierce had pointed out that if he was so damn determined to be a father, he'd need to buy a car seat.

"Give her to me," the bossy waitress said. "And go get her diapers and clothes. She's probably one of those babies who doesn't like being wet."

Will opened his mouth to protest, but by that time the kid was out of his arms and into Daisy's. And the little girl stopped screaming. "How'd you do that?"

"Just get the diapers, cowboy." She rubbed the baby's back. "We'll work on your education later."

No fool, Will Rogers Wilson did as he was told.

2

BARLOW STUCK his head out of the kitchen. "Hey, Daize! Your order's up!"

"For crying out loud, Barlow, can't you see I'm busy here?"

"But—"

"Yell like that again," Daisy said, "and you'll be back living in your van."

The cook wasn't impressed with the threat. "You don't scare me. That van and I understand each other."

Heather hurried past and slapped another order on the counter. She looked back at Daisy and the baby. "Now I've seen everything."

"I've held plenty of babies," Daisy muttered, sitting on the stool at the end of the counter. She surveyed the room and noticed four booths had filled. Well, they could wait a few extra minutes. It wouldn't hurt anyone.

"What a little sweetheart," Mrs. Anderson cooed, pausing on her way to a table to join her friends from church. "Look, Hazel," she said, gesturing to an elderly woman with a cane who was slowly making her way across the room. "Isn't she a little sweetheart?"

Daisy turned the baby in her arms so the ladies could admire her and the little sweetheart herself turned her wide-eyed gaze on the two gray-haired women. "I think she likes people," Daisy told them.

"Well, she sure seems to," Maude Anderson agreed. "We need more babies in town. Has Jane Pierce had hers yet?"

"No. Joe was in here just a few minutes ago and said they were still waiting."

Heather leaned over the counter. "Speaking of waiting, we have four booths I haven't gotten to yet."

Daisy ignored the hint. She helped the baby wave bye-bye to Maude and her friend as the ladies joined their friends at one of the center tables that seated six.

"This is really weird. I'd never have believed one baby could turn you into such a pushover." Heather picked up an armload of plastic-coated menus and hurried past her boss.

"I could use a refill," said the rancher seated next to Daisy. He pushed his empty coffee mug a couple of inches in Daisy's direction.

She couldn't help glaring at him. "Can't a woman sit down for a minute?"

"Uh, no hurry, then." He looked down at the baby. "Is that yours?"

"No." The door jangled again and Billy, his arms loaded with plastic shopping bags, entered the restaurant. "It's his," she said, gesturing toward the cowboy.

"His?"

"Unfortunately." Daisy slipped off the stool and carried the baby to her father, who dropped the bags in front of the booth.

"All set," he said, brushing snowflakes from his coat. He glanced over at the row of men who had swiveled around on their stools to stare at him. "It's really snowing now," he announced, as if anybody was interested in the weather.

"Looks like we're gonna get hit pretty hard," one of the men agreed. "How're things out at the ranch?"

"I'm making progress," Billy said. "It's an old place and it sure needs a lot of work."

"I hear you," one of the other ranchers said as Billy shrugged off his coat.

"I think I got everything." He grinned at both of them, and Daisy was struck by the laugh lines that fanned from the corners of his blue eyes. He looked older than she'd originally thought.

"Billy, how old is this child?"

"I don't know. Two months, the doc said." He dug into one of the bags and pulled out a sack of disposable diapers. "And call me Will. I'm not rodeoin' anymore. Do you think these are going to be all right?"

Daisy checked the size. "They should be. Good, you got those nice tabs. Isn't that nice that we don't have to use pins anymore?"

"I've broken too many fingers to be good with pins," Will agreed, rummaging through another bag. This time he displayed a box of baby wipes. "Joe said these were important."

"I think you and—what's her name?"

"I don't know."

"Oh. So I guess I'd better not ask where her mother is?"

Will didn't answer, but the look in his eyes let her know she'd hit a nerve. So a woman had left him with the baby. What kind of person could do that? Well, considering Billy's reputation, she supposed he'd been with all kinds of women. Most likely this baby's mother had moved on to another rodeo star.

"Well, what do you know about this baby?"

"Look, lady, I know I'm taking care of her until—" He stopped talking and ripped open the top of the plastic bag of diapers.

"Until?"

"Never mind."

Daisy held the baby so that the child's head was nestled against her neck. She'd almost forgotten that warmth, that sweet satisfaction that came from holding a tiny baby in her arms. It was best not to get used to it, though. "Here," Daisy said, handing him the child. "I have to go back to work. Are you sure you know how to change a diaper?"

"I've done it a couple of times now."

"Then that makes you an expert," she agreed, looking at the bags of supplies. She couldn't help being impressed. At least the cowboy was willing to part with some money on behalf of this baby. "Did Joe help you buy all this?"

"Yeah. Uh, Daisy, where do I do it?"

"Lay her down on the bench and change her there. She's just wet, that's all."

"I hope." His voice was grim as he lay the baby down. "At least she's not screaming at me anymore."

Daisy took a step backward. Barlow was yelling for her again and customers were calling Heather. "When you're done, bring her to me and I'll hold her while you wash up. Your dinner's ready when you are." She shouldn't feel sympathy for him. After all, he'd gotten himself into this mess. He'd had his fun and a child had been conceived. Daisy turned her back on the cowboy and vowed to mind her own business from now on.

She'd already made enough mistakes with men in her life. And if she had a dollar for every dirty diaper she'd changed, well, she wouldn't be running a restaurant seven days a week.

"I'm coming," she scolded over the noisy conversations around her. Barlow gave her a thumbs-up sign and turned back to the grill. She was going to start taking some time off, she promised herself. Just as soon as she figured out if she was making any money or not.

THE WAITRESS, Daisy Something, was right. The baby needed a name. He couldn't keep thinking of her as "Sarah's baby." The screaming child with the big blue eyes spurting tears like a spring waterfall needed a name. Even Daisy, a woman with no kids and a skillet for a heart, recognized that much.

Will gave up trying to eat his meat loaf. He had no stomach for food, anyway. How could he, when Sarah was out there somewhere? And once again, he couldn't find her. He wondered if that was why the baby was putting up such a fuss. Did babies know when their mothers weren't around?

"You need help," Daisy said, sliding into the seat across from him. She plopped two large paper bags on the table.

"I think you've said that before." He lifted the baby across the table and into Daisy's outstretched arms. "How do you know so much about kids?"

She patted the baby softly on the back and ignored the question. "I think your little girl is tired. She needs her bed and a quiet room. I guess it's too much to hope that you have a rocking chair?"

"I don't even have a bed for her."

"Fatherhood caught you by surprise, I take it."

Will thought of waking up to a baby in a basket on his doorstep. "You wouldn't believe it if I told you."

"How are you going to take care of a baby?"

"You think I can't because I'm a man?"

"Because you're Billy Wilson, a cowboy with a reputation for running wild. Not exactly the paternal type."

"Will, remember? And you know this because..."

"People talk."

"Yeah, well, the people in this town always have."

"I guess you keep giving them reasons."

"Her name is Spring," he decided. Like that dream he'd had this morning, where he'd been counting calves and working in his shirtsleeves.

"Look, I know I'm being a pain, but don't you have any idea where her mother is?"

"No. But I'll find her. Soon."

"And if she doesn't want to be found?"

"I'll find her," he repeated, knowing that wherever she was, Sarah needed him more than she ever had.

"Tell you what," Daisy said. "Why don't you take these hamburgers and fries over to the Pierces' house while I calm down little Spring. She seems to like walking around with me and you look like you could use some air."

He could use a whiskey, but he'd settle for driving a few blocks in a Montana snow squall. "You sure?"

"I'm sure. While you're there, look pitiful and act charming and ask Jane if you can borrow something for Spring to sleep in, just for tonight. Tomorrow you can go to North Bend and buy a crib."

He started to thank her, but she interrupted him. "Don't take all afternoon, either," she said. "I think I'm going to close up early."

"SOMEONE LEFT YOU a baby?"

"I know, I know. Joe already did the double take.

So did I." Will smiled the smile that Jane knew drove most of the women in town just a little bit crazy. The young ones thought of what luscious possibilities were in store, while the older ones remembered what it was like to be young and all heated up.

"Sit," Jane ordered, managing to lower herself onto a living-room chair without tipping it over. "Tell me everything."

"You haven't heard from Joe?" He moved a toy truck out of the way and sat down on the couch.

"Just a message from the dispatcher. They're up to their ears out on the interstate. A semi loaded with hogs tipped over."

"I guess the storm was worse than I thought."

"I don't want to talk about the weather, Will. Tell me about the baby."

"I can't stay very long. The woman at the café is taking care of her until I get back. You don't mind lending me something for her to sleep in?"

"I have more stuff than I know what to do with," she assured him. "What woman at the café?"

"The waitress. Daisy."

"She owns the place, you know."

Will shrugged. "Whatever. She knew how to get the baby to stop yelling at me."

"She did?" The woman didn't seem like the type, though she'd always been nice to the boys when Janie treated them to lunch. "You said Daisy offered to watch the baby?"

"Yeah. Why?"

Jane struggled to lean against the back of Joe's leather recliner. "I don't know. I guess I never pictured her with kids."

"She had a lot to say about how to take care of babies."

Janie laughed. "And you prefer the quiet type?"

Will fidgeted with his hat. "I'm not looking for a woman."

"But they're always looking for you," Janie pointed out, pleased to have company on such a miserable Sunday. The boys, settled in the kitchen with their hamburger dinner, were finally worn out from playing in makeshift tents all day. And Jane was grateful for adult company. "Who's the mother?"

"Who's the father?"

"Not you?"

He shook his head. "Not that anyone will believe me."

"This is true." So there was more to the story, and Will Wilson wasn't going to talk about it.

"Don't you want to eat?" Clearly her handsome guest was anxious to leave, but Janie wasn't ready to let him go just yet. She didn't want to admit that she hated to be alone right now. These last couple of weeks had crawled by so agonizingly slowly.

"Not right now. I can only eat a few bites at a time anyway." She looked down at her bulging abdomen. "There's not much room in there for food."

Will frowned. "Do you think she's all right?"

"Anyone can take care of a baby for a few—"

"I mean the baby's mother," he said, swallowing hard as he gazed at Janie. He looked like someone who'd had a hard day, too.

"I guess there's no way to know that."

"What would make a woman leave her kid?"

"I really can't imagine," she answered, wishing she could think of some way to make him feel better. She didn't know him well, but she knew that Joe liked and respected him. Their friendship went back a long way. "But whatever made her leave her baby, at least she left her with someone who would take good care of her."

Will took a deep breath. "I guess she could have dumped her in a gas-station bathroom or something. You hear those stories on the news."

"But she didn't."

"No. She wouldn't do that."

"Then you know who she is?"

The infuriating cowboy didn't answer her question. Instead he stood and fidgeted with his hat. "Is there anything I can do before I leave? I could bring some wood in, fix the fire or something."

"That would be a big help," Janie said, trying to maneuver her awkward body out of the chair. "I'll get the bassinet."

"Just tell me where it is," Will said, giving her a hand as he frowned down at her. "Maybe you shouldn't be moving around too much."

"I'm having trouble getting around today."

"Yeah." He grinned. "I can see that."

"Don't laugh. You'll get married someday and

have all this to deal with." She gestured toward the braided rug covered with Matchbox cars and Lego.

"No, ma'am," he drawled, putting his Stetson on. "I'm not the marrying kind."

"Until this morning you weren't the fatherly kind, either." And until fifteen minutes ago Jane would have bet that Daisy McGregor didn't have a maternal bone in her well-endowed body, either. "I think this is going to be an interesting winter," Jane declared, panting a little as she made her way across the room. "Follow me, Daddy."

She turned in time to see the cowboy wince.

"I WILL NOT fall in love with you," Daisy told the baby she held against her chest. "I don't care how adorable you are. Or how tiny. Or how sweet." She walked over to the door and flipped the sign over to say Closed to any passersby. Though with the amount of snow that was coming down now, Daisy couldn't imagine why even intrepid Montanans would venture out for a meat loaf special. Daisy switched the outside lights off and turned back to the restaurant to count how many tables were still occupied.

Barlow waved his approval, but Heather continued to pour coffee for a table of six. Daisy watched the young woman plop the bill down and scurry off to another table of dessert-eating ranchers and their wives.

She wished everyone would go home. She wished this baby would go home, though heaven only knew what was in store for her tonight. And tomorrow. And the day after that.

It is none of my business, Daisy reminded herself, absently planting a kiss on top of the baby's downy head.

"Daisy, did you really close?"

"Yes. There's a storm and—"

"Cool," Heather said, lifting the back of her hair off her neck. "I've got a date."

"But the storm—"

"Oh, that's okay. It's not like we're going anywhere, just to his house."

Daisy pointed to the baby. "You do know where these come from, don't you?"

"Unlike some people around here." She grinned. "My mother's already given me that lecture."

"Good for your mother."

"Hey, I'm only nineteen. And there's no way I want one of these little rug rats, that's for sure."

"Even more reason to listen to your mother."

"I hate to interrupt all this advice, but your boyfriend's back," Heather said, motioning toward the door. "Look."

Daisy turned and sure enough, Will Wilson entered the room. Snow covered his hat and shoulders, and he halted to stomp his feet on the rubber mat just inside the door. "He's not my boyfriend," she said, keeping her voice low.

"He will be, if you hang around him too long," the younger woman warned. "He's just that type, you know?"

"Yes," Daisy said, holding the baby close. She knew the type all too well. She'd married two of them.

Will still didn't think Daisy was the maternal-looking type, not with that curly yellow hair and a body that a movie star would envy. No, Daisy wasn't the type he'd have figured for baby-sitting, but little Spring looked as content as could be in the waitress's arms. If he didn't know better, he'd swear both females looked disappointed when he walked into the restaurant.

"I got a bed," was all he could think of to say. Damn, he usually didn't get tongue-tied, but then again, this hadn't started out as a normal day.

"Good." Daisy plopped the baby into his arms. "You'd better wrap her up and get on your way before the storm gets worse."

"It's already tapering off." Spring protested when a snowflake from his coat brushed her cheek. "But I guess I should get on my way."

"I guess," she agreed.

"You could come, too." She didn't look impressed, so Will added, "Just kidding. Sort of."

"You'll be fine. You have enough formula?"

"Plenty." Spring began to wail, heartbreaking cries that made every diner in the restaurant turn their heads in Will's direction as if they thought he'd pinched the kid or something.

"Maybe she'll sleep in the car on the way home." But even Daisy looked doubtful as her gaze met Will's.

"You think?"

"I hope so." She raised her voice over the sound of the baby. "For your sake."

"Well," he hesitated. "Thanks for the help."

"Sure. I hope you find her mother soon."

"Yeah. Me, too."

"What?"

He raised his voice. "Me, too!"

A group of elderly ladies making their way to the door stopped to frown at him. "You don't have to yell at her, Billy."

"I wasn't—"

Maude put one arthritic finger to her lips. "Shh."

The other women nodded approvingly. Will turned back to the waitress.

"Look," he said, feeling more desperate than he ever had in his thirty-two years. "I'll do anything, pay anything, if you'll come home with me."

Daisy laughed.

Will didn't. "I mean it. I've got to hire someone, but I'm not going to find anyone on a Sunday afternoon in the middle of a storm, not in this town."

"I have a business to run."

"She likes you." He turned the baby so she faced Daisy.

"You don't play fair, do you?"

"Never."

"Go home with him," Heather said, sweeping past with the coffeepot. "You're closing up anyway."

"You are?" At last, his situation was improving.

He plopped the baby back into Daisy's arms. "Come on, I've got the truck all warmed up."

"I'm not going anywhere," the woman repeated. But she settled Spring against her and tucked the baby's head under her chin. "Especially not to your house."

"Ranch," he corrected. "Five miles north of town."

"Good for you," she said, patting the baby's back. "All right, I'll keep her for tonight." She looked very serious, which made Will want to smile. "But just for one night. You obviously don't know what you're doing with this poor little thing."

"You mean it?"

She took a deep breath. "Bring in the bed. I live around back."

"In Ralph's old apartment?"

"It's been renovated," she said, looking down at the baby. "I must be out of my mind."

Will didn't argue. From the minute he'd seen the baby he'd felt the same way.

3

"I DON'T KNOW WHY I'm doing this," Daisy muttered. She opened the door to her apartment and the cowboy carried in a blue bassinet.

"You're a sucker for babies," Will said. "Just like me." He stomped the snow off his boots before entering the kitchen, she noticed. Someone had taught him manners.

"You're supposed to be a sucker for your own child," Daisy said, still cradling the child in her arms. "I don't have that excuse."

"You don't have any kids?"

"No. Follow me."

She led him into the living room, a long rectangle that held the remains of two marriages and what she'd inherited from her grandmother.

"Nice place." He set the bassinet on the floor. "Doesn't look at all like it did when Ralph was having poker games back here."

"Thank goodness for that." She was proud of the one-bedroom apartment, pleased with the exposed log wall at one end of the living room. She liked her white walls and flowered rugs and elegant cherry coffee tables. Yet Daisy would bet that Ralph had made a lot more money in the gambling business back here than she did serving hamburgers and eggs out in front.

"Well, yeah. It smells better, too," he said, peering at the collection of photographs on a shelf over the sofa. "Who are all these people?"

"Family," Daisy said, wishing he'd mind his own business. "You'll have to get the rest of—"

"They sure look like a serious bunch." He turned around and smiled at her. "Is that where you get it from?"

"You can save the personal questions for later. Right now you'd better go get the rest of Spring's belongings from the restaurant." She started to urge him out the door where he'd come in, but he stopped short.

"There's a door over there that connects to the storage room and then goes right out to the kitchen, you know."

"I know, but I'd rather not have anyone see you going in and out of my house."

"I just did."

"That's different. The front door just seems more, I don't know, acceptable."

"So in order to protect your, uh, reputation I'm supposed to go out in the snow, around the corner, in the front door, grab the bags and then head out again?"

"Exactly. Unless you'd just rather take this baby home tonight."

"Without you?"

"Absolutely."

"You play rough, sweetheart." Again, that charming flash of a smile lit his face. "Okay, you win. Out the front door it is." He touched the baby's cheek with one finger and gazed down at her with an adoring expression. "I suppose a little more snow won't hurt me." He glanced up at Daisy. "I'll be back."

Daisy followed him out to the kitchen and watched him from the window over the sink. The sky had darkened considerably, streetlights were shining through the snow and the trees that lined the school playground across the street bent in the wind. Billy—Will—hunched over, hurried past the building and disappeared around the corner.

Daisy looked down at the baby, whose big blue eyes didn't look the least bit sleepy. "Your daddy wants to take good care of you, you know."

Spring didn't blink, but one tiny fist moved.

"But where is your mommy, honey? We sure would like to know." In fact, Daisy wasn't sure at all as she went back into the living room and sat in her grandmother's oak rocking chair. What kind of woman would leave her little baby at Billy Wilson's ranch? She'd taken a big risk, all right. The man could have been sleeping somewhere else on a Saturday night and not even have been home Sunday morning to welcome his baby. Or he could have had Sheriff Pierce deliver the child to some child-welfare agency. He could have said "Not mine" and never be faced with changing diapers or heating bottles or being nice to overworked waitresses.

But he hadn't. Which didn't go along with his reputation at all. Unless he loved the baby's mother and thought this baby would be the connection between them. If she did know who that woman was, she'd sit her down and give her a good piece of her mind. Imagine abandoning a little baby. What on earth had that woman been thinking? Daisy rocked the baby gently until Spring's eyes closed. Until the opening of the back door and the stomping of cowboy boots almost caused her to open them again.

Daisy was torn between scolding the cowboy or keeping still and hoping Spring wouldn't waken. It didn't stop her from glaring at him when he entered the room with fistfuls of plastic shopping bags. "You have to be quiet," she whispered. "I just got her to sleep."

He stepped closer and they both looked at Spring's closed eyelids. "She still looks pretty sleepy to me," he said. "Where should I put this stuff?"

"Anywhere," she said. "Just be quiet doing it."

He dropped them where he stood, taking care not to let the plastic make more than a quiet rustling sound. "Now what?"

"Can you boil water?"

"Sure," he gulped. "What are we going to do?"

"You're going to make tea," she explained. "And I'm going to try to get your daughter to sleep in her bed."

"Good plan." He took off his jacket and draped it over the back of an overstuffed chair, then put his hat on top of it. "Uh, you wouldn't have anything stronger?"

"There's whiskey in the cupboard to the right of the sink." She hesitated. "You're not going to get drunk, are you?" He looked puzzled. "I've heard the stories," she explained. "You're a regular legend around here."

He glared at her. "I am not going to get drunk. But I sure as hell don't mind a swallow of whiskey on a cold January night."

"Then be my guest."

"Forget it. You want tea? I'll make tea." He disappeared into the kitchen and Daisy heard the water running and the kettle bang on the top of the stove. Then cupboard doors squeaked open and shut until Daisy figured he'd found the mugs and tea bags. Daisy closed her eyes and rocked for a few long minutes while her feet burned and her legs ached from working since five-thirty that morning. She'd been glad for the excuse to close up early. She hoped her plans for a pizza business would make enough money so she wouldn't have to work seven days a week. She wanted to stay here in this town, wanted to put down roots and make a life for herself. She wanted to grow old here, surrounded by people she'd known for years. She wanted to make friends, meet a nice man, have a few nice children.

But first, this baby who'd been jostled around by strangers all day was going to sleep in a bed. Daisy smiled to herself when she heard a muffled curse come from the kitchen. The baby's father had a lot to learn, too, but that could wait. She'd drink her tea and put the baby to sleep and then she'd take a quick shower to wash the smell of deep-fryer grease from her hair.

Daisy kept her eyes closed and rocked gently for long, relaxing moments until she heard Will set a cup on the table.

"Thanks," she whispered, blinking at him as she stopped the rocker.

He kept his voice low. "No problem."

Daisy saw that the little girl was still asleep. "I'm going to try to put her to bed," she whispered, easing herself out of the chair. She tiptoed over the couch and laid Spring on her back before adjusting the pink blanket around her.

So far so good, Daisy thought, tiptoeing back to pick up her tea. She motioned to Will to follow her into the kitchen.

"I think she'll sleep for a while," she told him as she sat at the tiny table that was just big enough for one person. "She just needed a quiet place."

"Yeah. It's been one hell of a day." He leaned against the counter and crossed his arms in front of his chest.

"You'd better get some rest," she said.

"Not yet," he said. "Can I use this phone?"

"Sure, but—" She stopped as he lifted the receiver from the wall. How could she tell this stranger that she wanted him to leave so she could shower while his baby slept? "Look, Will, she's not going to sleep for more than an hour or two, so I think you should—"

Too late. He'd turned around to talk into the receiver. "Joe? Any luck?" Silence. "No problem. Tell her the baby's sleeping in it right now. Yeah. Tomorrow." He hung up the phone and turned to face Daisy again. "No luck finding who left Spring with me. A semi accident on the interstate kept Joe busy for hours."

"What did you expect him to do?"

"Look for a young woman in an old truck with a bad muffler."

"You know who she is?"

"I have a pretty good hunch. What were you saying about the baby sleeping?"

"Oh." She sipped her tea. He hadn't put sugar in it, but she didn't have the energy to get up and get the sugar bowl from the counter. "You should go home now. Can you be back here at six? I have to open up before that, but I can bring her out front with me for a little while."

"Go home?"

"Well, that's the general plan. I'm hoping she'll sleep for a few hours now. She's going to want to eat every three or four hours and I can sleep in between—"

"I'm not leaving her," Will said.

"You can't take her out in the cold, either. It's not good for her."

"But I can't leave her," he repeated, folding his

arms in front of his chest again. "That wasn't the plan."

"It was my plan," she insisted, wondering what in the world was the matter with him. "You didn't think you were staying here, too, did you?"

He nodded. "For baby lessons."

"Baby lessons?"

"You said you were going to teach me how to take care of her."

"Not tonight."

"Daisy, who else can I ask? Joe is busy with cop work, Janie can barely get up from a chair, and the rest of the town thinks I'm either a drunk or a rodeo stud."

She couldn't disagree with that. "A rodeo stud who now has a baby to care for. Go home and get some rest."

He didn't budge. "You said I've got a lot to learn."

"You know diapers, bottles and burping already." Lord, her feet ached and now her head was joining in the torture. "Go home and I'll teach you the rest tomorrow."

"Honey, I can't leave her. Not now, when I just got her."

"You can't stay here. Everyone will see your truck parked outside."

"It's parked around the corner, at the gas station. It'll look like it needs work."

"I should have minded my own business."

Will crossed the space between them in one

stride. He leaned on the table and smiled into her eyes. "Now, honey, what kind of fun is that?"

"Don't 'honey' me." Daisy leaned her head on her hand and studied the man determined to spend the night in her house. He was handsome, but he was a little crazy, too. The charming cowboys always were.

"SWEETHEART, please don't look at me like that," he pleaded, looking down into a pair of tear-filled blue eyes.

Spring paid no attention. Instead she opened her mouth even wider and howled loud enough to wake the dead. Will knew he was in one hell of a jam here. He could hear the shower running at the other end of the small apartment, so Daisy was going to be no help at all. He didn't know whether to hope she heard the baby's cries and would come and rescue them both, or to hope that she heard nothing and would think he was approaching some kind of competence with a thick wad of paper diaper. How did anything so bulky end up on the bottom half of a baby? Especially a baby whose legs kicked and arms flailed as if she were trying to stay on a championship bull.

"I'm doing the best I can," he said, trying not to scrape her soft belly with his callused fingers. His left thumb, which had been broken more times than he could remember, managed to tape one side of the diaper pretty much the way Joe had showed him. He was working on the right side when he heard

Daisy turn off the shower water. Damn, he was going to hear it now. It hadn't been the best evening of his life. Daisy acted like he was the kind of cowboy who left hordes of pregnant women in every town after every rodeo. Hell, there'd been some nights he'd been so busted up that the only women who'd looked good were the nurses carrying pain pills.

"When you're big enough, I'll give you any horse you want," he promised Spring, taping the other side. Too loose, but good enough. He scooped the baby into his arms and tucked her blanket around her so she wouldn't get cold, though Daisy had turned the heat up to about seventy-nine degrees. If it got any hotter in here, he'd be looking around for a margarita stand.

"How about a nice little bay? Or even one of those showy palominos all the girls seem to like so much? Anything you want, baby, just as long as you stop crying before Daisy comes out here and chews into me again."

Spring didn't seem to care about horses, so Will figured she was hungry again. Hell, she hadn't eaten in three whole hours. He hurried into the kitchen and pulled a bottle out of the refrigerator where Daisy had stored them. Efficient woman, he'd say that for her, though her sharp tongue didn't make her the kind of woman a man longed to have sitting by the fireside with him.

In bed would be a different matter, he decided, scrounging through scrupulously neat cabinets until he found a pan. He turned on the faucet and waited for hot water to fill the pan. That woman had a body that would knock a man clean off his feet. A man could lose himself for days in those breasts alone. Not him, however. He was a temporary father to a baby who would someday be inspiring lust in the local boys and he would have to shoot every single one of those young men if they even so much as looked at her below her chin.

Spring's sobs continued, though she lowered the volume a few decibels when she heard the water running. He waited for Daisy to come out and take over, but so far she hadn't marched in and chewed him out. If he could get the milk heated and the bottle in Spring's mouth, he'd be home free. He lifted the bottle out of the water, wiped it on his sleeve, shook a few drops on his arm and pronounced it ready to eat. Spring saw it and opened her mouth to scream, but Will was one step ahead of her.

"You're as greedy as Sarah was," he told her, watching her suck down the milk. He should have taken better care of Sarah, but she wasn't the type to listen to advice. He couldn't think about her without worrying his heart right out of his chest, so Will tried hard not to think about where Sarah was and why she'd left her little girl behind.

"Who is Sarah?" Will turned to see Daisy standing in the doorway. A pink fuzzy robe covered her from neck to ankle, but she smelled like roses and looked like something out of *Playboy* magazine with all that yellow hair fluffed over her shoulders. She looked younger, too, with her face scrubbed of makeup and her cheeks pink from the shower.

"Huh?"

"Sarah." She looked at the baby and reached over and tucked the blanket securely around her bottom. "What have you done to her? She's not wearing anything but her diaper."

"That sleep thing was wet."

"She'll catch cold."

"She's breaking into a sweat," he insisted. "It's hotter than hell in here."

"You hear that wind?"

He listened to the typical Montana winter sound. "So?"

"I don't want her to be in any drafts." Daisy stepped closer and felt the baby's forehead as she watched her suck on the bottle. "It looks like you've figured out how to feed her."

"We're doing okay." He couldn't help sounding proud. So far Spring hadn't choked or dripped. He eased the nipple out of her mouth and set the bottle on the counter while he moved Spring to a vertical position. "I think I've figured out burping, too."

"Congratulations."

"Thanks." Spring obligingly burped by his collar and then hollered in his ear. He had the bottle back in her mouth in less than four seconds.

Daisy looked at the wall clock hanging above the refrigerator. "It's almost eight o'clock. I'll help you get her dressed and in bed, then we'd both better get some sleep. Whose going to take the first shift?"

"I will." He hadn't missed the shadows under her eyes or the way she'd tried to hide her yawn when she thought he was busy burping Spring. "What time do you usually get up in the morning?"

"Around five."

He winced. "That's even early for a rancher."

"It takes me a while to wake up," she admitted. "I'd like to find someone for the morning shift, but I haven't had any luck."

He followed her into the living room and watched while she opened packages of baby paraphernalia and laid out a one-piece yellow thing that looked like long underwear. Then she left the room and returned with a pile of bedding.

"You sleep here," she said, dumping the blankets and pillow on top of the cushions.

"Where should we put Spring?"

"Are you a light sleeper?"

"No." He couldn't help smiling. "Which is why I didn't wake up in time to see who left this kid with me."

"Oh. Then we'll put the bassinet beside the couch."

He pulled the empty bottle away from the baby, who immediately complained. "I don't think I'll have any trouble hearing her, though. She's got one hell of a voice."

"She does seem to have a temper," Daisy agreed. "Like Sarah?"

"Yeah," he admitted, struggling to put the baby

to his shoulder while the blanket was wrapped around his wrist. "Just like Sarah."

"Don't worry." Daisy lifted the child from his arms. "I'm not going to ask any more questions." She tucked the baby against her and cooed into her ear until Spring stopped fussing. "You're allowed your secrets."

"Secrets? Never had any, not in this town," he said, suddenly exhausted. "Everyone will be talking about this tomorrow morning."

"No one will dare," Daisy promised, kissing the baby's head. "Not while they're drinking my coffee."

She really was one hell of a good-looking woman. Too bad she preferred babies to cowboys.

"HOW'S THAT?" Joe tucked another pillow against Janie's spine so she was comfortable on her side in the king-size bed.

"Great, thanks." She gave him a smile that she hoped was convincing. Truth was, her back hurt like hell and her feet were swollen to the size of footballs, but she didn't want Joe to worry. He worried too much as it was. "Tell me more about Will's baby. Does he know who the mother is?"

"He might." Joe didn't look at her, which meant he knew more than he was telling.

"Do you think you can find her?"

"I'm trying." He sat on the edge of the bed with his back to her while he unbuttoned his shirt and tossed it on a chair.

Jane tried a new approach. "How is he going to take care of a baby all by himself? Maybe he should bring it over here tomorrow, so I can see—"

"You're not doing anything but staying off your feet," her husband declared. "And Will has plenty of help. He's most likely at Daisy McGregor's right now."

There were definitely advantages being married to the deputy sheriff. "How do you know that?"

"His truck's parked at Hal's."

"Maybe it's broken."

"He bought it new two months ago." Joe slid into bed and got under the blankets. "God, it's a cold night. You want the light on?"

"No. You think he's spending the night with her? That was fast." She knew Will was a charmer with a reputation, but she didn't know he could work magic. Daisy McGregor had been in town six months and she hadn't dated once. Some said it was because she wasn't really divorced. Jane, who had waitressed one summer in Bozeman, figured it was because the woman was too darn tired.

"It's the baby," Joe said, switching the room into darkness. "She's the only one who could get it to stop crying." He sighed. "And I don't know if he's spending all night. It's just a hunch."

"You have good hunches."

"Um."

"She doesn't have any kids."

"Nope."

"And she's been divorced. Twice."

"So?"

"So I guess someone like Will isn't going to surprise her. Or break her heart."

"Um."

She prodded his calf with her big toe. "Don't go to sleep yet. Please?"

He opened his eyes. "What? You feeling okay?"

"Fine. I just can't believe he's sleeping with her."

Joe chuckled. "He's not tonight. But he will."

"You think?"

"Yeah." He closed his eyes again and pulled the blankets around his neck.

"Why?"

No answer. Jane nudged him with her foot once again, but gently. After all, the man had been rescuing hogs all afternoon and hauling two teenagers out of a ditch this evening. She really should be nicer to him—but then again, he wasn't the one carrying around twenty-five extra pounds of baby in front of him all day long. "I like Will," she told her dozing husband. "But any woman with any sense knows he's trouble."

4

JUST BECAUSE Will took the first shift didn't mean that Daisy fell asleep right away. She heard the man walking around, running the water in the bathroom, talking in a low murmur on the phone. She assumed he was talking to the sheriff again, trying to find the mysterious Sarah. Daisy lay in her double bed and listened to the sound of another person in her home. She didn't know whether she liked it or not, though she knew she would sleep better if the house was silent, if she wasn't listening for the baby's cry in the night. She didn't really think Billy Wilson could handle this, which was why she now had company and couldn't sleep. It was her own fault. She had invited a baby and had gotten stuck with a cowboy.

A cowboy who was a stranger. She'd locked the bedroom door, just in case. And she told herself that any friend of Joe Pierce's wouldn't be an insane criminal who walked around tricking innocent women with an abandoned-baby story. Her imagination was working overtime, and she knew she should be sleeping. The midnight feeding would come soon enough, unless Spring was one of those babies who slept until dawn.

Daisy snuggled under the covers and tried to think about next week's steak special. Which night should it be? And how to increase the supper business, which should be more profitable. Breakfast was always busy, but it wasn't a big moneymaker. A customer could sit for two hours and drink a dollar cup of coffee, with all the refills he could stomach. The lunch soup specials were good business, but only because Barlow's secret chili recipe was the stuff of legend. Then there were the ever-popular chili dogs. Daisy sighed into the darkness. The Cowman's Café was probably single-handedly responsible for the high cholesterol count of every rancher in northeast Montana.

The house was silent now, giving Daisy no excuse to toss and turn under two pink blankets and a burgundy-rose print comforter. She wouldn't have minded having the baby in the bassinet beside her. It wouldn't have been the first time she'd gone to sleep listening to a child's soft breathing. And it wouldn't be the last time she'd lie awake in the night wondering if she'd be alone for the rest of her life. The eldest daughter of six, she had grown up knowing a lot about kids and nothing at all about men, except what to feed them.

THE ALARM CLOCK woke her before the baby did, though Daisy heard the child's hungry cries on the other side of the bedroom door. She shut off her alarm and saw that it was five o'clock already; she'd slept through the night. She grabbed her robe and wrapped it around her before hurrying out to the living room. The place looked as if a tornado had hit it, with blankets lumped on the couch and baby things strewn on the carpet. She heard Will in the kitchen.

"Honey pie, you just have to cut Uncle Will some slack."

Spring didn't stop crying, so Daisy hurried into the kitchen and took the baby from Will's arms. "Here," she said. "Let me help."

"I'm trying to heat this up as fast as I can," he said, looking rumpled. His day-old growth of whiskers gave him a sexy look, and his shirt was unbuttoned to reveal a very wide and very muscular chest. Daisy looked away and talked to the baby.

"Your daddy's doing a good job," she cooed, bouncing the child gently to distract her from the sight of the bottle in the sink.

"Not so good," he muttered, glancing at the baby. "Watch out."

"For what?"

"I think I got that diaper a little loose. I have more damn trouble with those sticky things," he grumbled, lifting the bottle from the water. He tested it on his hand with all the casual experience of a father of five.

"You're getting awfully good at that," she said, taking the bottle he handed her and shifting the baby so that she could drink. "Is that why you didn't wake me up?"

"Didn't seem right." Those dark sleepy eyes met hers. "My baby. My problem."

"But I thought you wanted help."

"Just knowing someone was around in case I needed some backup made a big difference," he assured her. "Would you mind feeding her while I take a quick shower?"

"Go ahead. There should be extra razors and toothbrushes in the bathroom closet."

"That's okay. I got my stuff out of the truck last night."

"Oh?"

He shrugged. "Old habit."

"Uh-huh." She couldn't help smiling, especially when she watched him pour her a cup of coffee from the glass carafe. He started to hand it to her and stopped.

"I'll wait," she said, "though it's a real treat to have someone else make the coffee."

"I couldn't sleep," he admitted. "I was afraid I wouldn't hear her if she woke up."

"Not hear this child?" Daisy laughed. "I think this one will always let you know what she wants." The baby's blue-eyed gaze never left Daisy's face. "I wonder who she thinks I am," she said. "She can't figure it out."

"She looks at me like that, too. Right before she yells." He ran his hand through his rumpled hair. "I'm not sure she likes me."

"She doesn't have much choice."

He winced. "Thanks."

"You know what I mean." She popped the half-empty bottle out of Spring's mouth and handed her to Will. "Burp," she said, reaching for the coffee. She took several careful sips of the strongest brew she'd ever tasted. He must have used three times more coffee than he needed to, or else these rodeo men were made of strong stuff. "How can you drink this?"

"I'm going to have a long day."

"Understatement of the winter, pal," she said, dumping a third of the coffee into the sink. She filled her mug with hot water from the faucet. "You'd better find a baby-sitter real fast."

"That's the plan." He took the bottle from the counter where Daisy had left it and continued to feed the baby. "Do you have any suggestions?"

She watched the baby stare up at Will. Her little legs dangled, completely relaxed as she placed her trust in the cowboy's strength. The diaper hung close to her knees, and if she decided to pee, most of it would run down Will's chest. "Give her to me and go get yourself cleaned up," she said, setting her coffee on the table. She held out her arms and Will transferred the baby into her embrace. But not without the backs of his fingers brushing against her breasts for one brief second. She told herself he hadn't done it on purpose. His quick exit from the kitchen probably meant he was as embarrassed as she was by the contact.

And she wore a thick robe and a flannel nightgown. The brush of the back of his hand against her was nothing. It shouldn't have tingled. Shouldn't still be tingling. And she certainly didn't need to feel such discomforting heat in her face. Daisy walked over to the thermostat and turned the heat down. It had gotten too hot in here, that was all.

HER BEDROOM DOOR was shut, but he heard her talking to the baby. He was beginning to learn that there was a certain voice that a woman used when she talked to an infant, a cheerful coochy-coo thing that would soon grate on a man's nerves.

And his were raw. He had an almost overwhelming urge to grab his coat and his car keys and head out the back door, to cross the ice-covered road, get in his truck and head west. He could do that, he told himself, surveying the very domestic chaos in Daisy's living room. Daisy would turn the baby over to Joe, who would turn her over to the authorities. She would be adopted eventually, and she would have a better home with two parents who actually knew what they were doing.

Damn, it was tempting. He went into the kitchen and with shaking hands emptied the last of the coffee into a rose-covered mug. The woman had flowers on everything: the sheets, the pillows, the plates, the walls. Even the bath towels were covered with flowers and scented like roses. It was enough to make a man want to run, even if he wasn't running away from fatherhood.

"You can stay here this morning for as long as you need to," Daisy said, coming up behind him.

He turned from the window and saw that she was dressed in her blue waitress outfit again. Her fluffy hair was piled up on top her head and she wore a gold chain around her neck. "I changed her diaper—you really have to get those tighter around her waist—and put new jammies on her. She'll probably play for a while if you leave her alone."

"Play?"

"Put her on her back in the bed and let her kick. She might like the exercise and you can go back to sleep for a while." Daisy held the baby at arm's length and popped her into his arms. "Thanks for letting me sleep, but I have to tell you that you really look like hell."

"Thanks."

"No, really, get some rest, okay?" She patted the baby's back. "Spring will be fine, won't you, sweetheart? Let Daddy have a little nap, okay?"

He didn't know how she could look so energetic at five forty-five. Maybe because she hadn't tried to fit a six-foot-two-inch frame on a five-foot-eight-inch couch. "Let me guess, you're a morning person, right?"

"How'd you guess?" She smiled, which was devastating to a man who hadn't had sex in over six months. "Get some rest and then come get some breakfast. And don't forget—"

"To come in the front door, not the back. I remember."

Her blue eyes were wide. "I don't want people to talk."

"No, we don't want that." He didn't dare tell her that despite his parking his truck at the gas station chances were the fact that he'd stayed here would be a topic of conversation this morning. He could have warned her that there was nothing anyone could do in this town without everyone knowing all the details and then some, but she didn't need to worry about it now. Not when she looked ready to greet the day. "Go on. I'll bet the Garvey brothers are waiting for you to unlock the door and turn on the lights."

"How'd you know that?"

He shrugged. "It's a small town."

She looked at her watch. "I'm late. There'll be hell to pay if the grill isn't hot by six." Daisy flew through the house and disappeared around the corner. He heard the door open and shut, and then he was alone. With Spring. He held her up to eye level as he walked into the living room.

"I will do anything, buy anything, pay anything if you will let me sleep for two hours." A bubble popped from between the baby's tiny pursed lips. "I'll take that to mean we have a deal?"

Will thought she might have smiled, but he couldn't be sure. He glanced towards the couch and knew he wouldn't get any sleep there. "Okay, then, how about stretching out in Mama Bear's bed?"

"DO YOU STILL HAVE HIM?" Joe settled himself on a stool and waited for someone to pour him a cup of coffee, which Daisy did.

"Shh," she said. "As far as I know, he and the baby have gone home. I left over four hours ago. How did you know he was at my place?"

He winked at her. "It's my business to know these things. I'm the sheriff."

"He called you," Daisy said, belatedly remembering that fact. "Have you found the baby's mother yet?"

The sheriff's face lost its teasing expression. "No. Needle in a haystack, too, since we're not talking about a recent birth. I've checked some area hospitals, but nothing's come back yet." He took a sip of coffee. "How'd he make out last night?"

"Just fine. He did it all by himself."

"Yeah, I thought he would."

"Why?"

Joe shrugged. "I've known Will all my life. He's never been afraid of anything."

"I guess that's why he was so good in the rodeo."

"Yeah, but fear didn't have anything to do with it." Joe smiled at her. "Can I get an order of eggs and bacon?"

"Sure. Fried?"

He nodded. "When he wakes up, tell him to come see me. We need to talk."

"Sure." Daisy ignored the curious look Heather gave her as she put the order on Barlow's clipboard.

"When he wakes up?" Heather said in a low voice. "Does this mean what I think it means? You spent the night there?"

"No." Daisy busied herself making another pot of coffee. "Of course not."

Heather sidled up next to her. "He spent the night with you?"

"He needed help with the baby. I couldn't let him try to take care of that poor little thing all by himself."

"Of course not. Just because he's the handsomest man this town has ever produced has nothing to do with it."

"Shut up," Daisy said, flicking the switch to On. "How was your date last night?"

"Not as exciting as yours. We just watched a movie."

"We fed a baby," Daisy countered, flashing her a quick smile.

"That's all?"

"Yep. Told you so."

Heather shook her head. "I'm the one saying 'I told you so,' boss. He's the kind of guy to get under your skin."

"He's not my type at all," she assured the girl, lying through her teeth. Will Wilson was exactly the kind of man she'd married twice before. Big mistakes.

"Who's not your type?" an elderly rancher called out. "You talking about me again, Daisy, sweetheart?"

"You're my type, Cal." She refilled his coffee, then went down the counter and topped off everyone's coffee while she was at it. "Old and rich."

"Well, old, anyway," Cal said, enjoying the attention of the other men seated at the counter.

"Hell, Cal," someone said. "You sold your biggest ranch to that movie star last year. You've got more money than the governor."

The men laughed, which was nothing new. They were a cheerful group in the morning, full of eggs and coffee and something to say. Sooner or later they'd put on their coats and wander off. Daisy often wondered what they did with the rest of their days. Some of them returned for lunch, others brought their wives for one of the dinner specials. But before ten, it was a man's world. She kept hoping that one of them would turn out to be the man for her, a kind and quiet man who wanted nothing more than a wife and kids. So far she had met a few possibilities, but the men who had asked her out on dates were not the men she hoped would ask her.

"Daize!"

She turned to see that Joe's order was up, so she delivered it to him. "Maybe I should check on your friend," she said, her voice low.

"No hurry," Joe said, picking up his fork and digging into a pile of hash browns. "If he's lucky enough to be asleep, leave him to it." He grinned. "At least for five minutes while I finish my breakfast."

"Take your time, Sheriff." A group of six sauntered in, so the morning rush wasn't over yet. "Maybe I've lucked out and he's already headed for home."

Joe's eyebrows rose. "Have you seen his place?"

"Of course not."

"Well, it's not what I'd call a 'home.'"

She picked up a handful of menus. "A ranch?"

He shook his head. "Will was going to burn it down at first, but my wife convinced him that it was worth saving and would add to the value of the place. I'm not sure she was right. That house needs a lot of work."

"Then why did he buy it?"

Joe picked up his coffee. "He didn't. He inherited it from his grandmother a few months ago. It's a nice piece of land and not too far from town."

Cal leaned over. "The Wilson place?"

"That's the one."

"Heard the grandson was back," the old man said, as Daisy hurried past to greet the new customers. "Those Wilson kids could get into more trouble than any kids I ever saw."

Daisy paused. "Kids?"

"Billy and his sister. Never knew what they would be up to, and the mother wasn't much help."

"Who?" the man to the right of Cal turned their direction.

"The Wilson kids, from north of town. Billy went on the rodeo circuit a while back." He looked at Joe. "When was that?"

"About fifteen years ago," the sheriff said, pushing his empty plate away. He pulled four dollars out of his pocket and put them on the counter. "Got a minute, Daisy?"

"Sure, just let me get these folks started."

"I'll do it," Heather said, plucking the menus from Daisy's hands. "One of them is real good-looking."

"Good luck." She turned to Joe and kept her voice low. "I'll meet you at the other door, otherwise people will—"

"Talk," he finished for her. "Yeah, I know. Thanks for breakfast." He nodded toward the rest of the men and left.

"Barlow? I'm taking a break," she called, untying her apron from around her waist. She tossed it under the counter and then went through the back room and unlocked the apartment door.

"Will?" Daisy tiptoed through the hall and into the living room, but there was no sign of the cowboy or his baby. Spring's belongings were as Daisy last saw them, stacked on chairs and spilling out of shopping bags, so she unlocked the back door for Joe.

"He must be here," she told him, knowing there was one room she hadn't checked. "Everything he bought is still in the living room."

Joe followed her down the short hallway. "Then where—"

"Here." Daisy gulped as she peered into her bedroom. Will looked much too comfortable stretched out on her bed. He was snoring quietly, his head on her pillow and Spring's little body tucked against his side. His unbuttoned shirt revealed a white T-shirt, his jeans were unsnapped and his feet were bare. The baby beside him kicked her legs and gurgled as if to say hello. "I guess he got tired of the couch."

"Well, tell him to call me when he wakes up."

"You're leaving?"

"I'll be at the office doing paperwork and making phone calls if you need me." He grinned. "I don't think Will is going to be much trouble, though."

"That's because he's not in your bed."

"He's slept on my couch a few times. You'll have one hell of a time waking him up."

No, she wouldn't. "Shouldn't he be on his ranch taking care of horses or cows or something?"

Joe chuckled. "See you later, Daisy. I'll let myself out."

Daisy tiptoed into the room and leaned over the bed to pick up Spring. "Hey, sweetheart. Did you have a nice nap?"

The cowboy didn't stir, not even when she shoved his leaden arm out of the way. She could raise her voice, but she didn't want to scare the baby. She could shake him, but that would involve touching him and she wasn't prepared to lay a hand on him. The more she kept her distance the better. Daisy settled for getting her bottle of water out of the bathroom closet and spraying his face with the mist.

"Shut the window, darlin'," he mumbled, and turned over on his stomach.

"Get up," she said, leaning close to his ear.

"Sorry, hon," he muttered. "Can't get it up now."

Daisy rolled her eyes heavenward. "Thank God for small mercies."

"WHERE IS SHE?"

Daisy, busy wiping the counter, looked up and glared at him. Too late he remembered he was supposed to go around and come in the restaurant door.

"She's fine," the waitress said. "No thanks to you."

"Where is she?" he repeated, hurrying to button his shirt as he crossed the room. "Did Sarah come—"

"Over there." Daisy pointed over his shoulder, so he turned to see his baby in the arms of that old witch Hazel Murphy and a boothful of her gossiping cronies. "See? She's fine."

He halted in mid-stride and turned back to Daisy. "Do you know what you've done?"

"Do you?"

Will stepped closer and leaned over the counter. "What in hell are you talking about?"

"You fell asleep—deeply asleep—while that baby was beside you. Awake. You can't do that." She scrubbed a piece of egg yolk from the Formica, then tossed the cloth into the sink. "It's not safe."

He sank onto the end stool. "Yeah. You're right." He glanced over his shoulder and saw the baby being passed to another old lady. The women were clearly enjoying themselves, and the baby didn't look like she minded the attention. Which proved she was a Wilson, of course. He turned back to Daisy, determined to apologize. "I guess I'm not used to fatherhood yet."

"No." She poured a cup of coffee and set it in front of him. "Here. Breakfast is over, but Barlow will make you some lunch."

"I'd better not. I have to see if Joe found out anything." But he took the coffee and remembered to say thank you. "Jeez, that scared me. Waking up and finding her gone like that..."

Daisy's eyes twinkled. "I guess that doesn't happen to you very often?"

"Yeah, right. Women usually beg me to stay." He tried to remember the last time that had happened, but his brain refused to cooperate. Not enough caffeine. Or not a good memory.

"Joe was here a couple of hours ago. He said to come over when you woke up."

"Did he say if he found anything?"

She shook her head. "Nothing. Sorry." Then she nodded towards the corner booth. "I fed her and cleaned her up, but I think your daughter is ready for another nap. She's been awake for a while and I can't leave—Heather has the afternoon off."

"I'll take her with me." He took one last swallow of coffee and stood. "I really appreciate the help you've given me."

"What about the ladies? Maybe one of them would baby-sit for you."

"And give them something else to talk about? No way in hell."

"Too late," Daisy whispered.

Sure enough, two hundred pounds of Mrs. Murphy were bearing down on him at high speed. "Billy Wilson," she called, adjusting her glasses. "Is that you?"

"Yes, ma'am."

"I heard you were back in town. Never thought I'd see the day that—"

"Excuse me, Mrs. Murphy, but I have to—"

"Oh, that girl of yours is just fine. Maude has her and we're all taking turns spoiling her silly. We didn't hear you got married. And you a father? Why you could have knocked me over with a feather when Daisy said that little baby was yours. Looks just like your mother, don't you think?"

He tried backing up, but the counter stopped him. "Yes, ma'am. Same eyes."

"Exactly what I told Maude. Same eyes, I said. And she's got your chin."

Will hoped to God that wasn't true. "I really have to get going," he said, moving sideways. "Spring, uh, needs a nap."

Hazel Murphy put a restraining hand on his arm and lowered her voice. "We're all real sorry about your wife. But you're better off without her, don't you think?" With that, she hurried off to rejoin her friends. Daisy handed him his hat and coat.

"I'll meet you around back with Spring," she said.

"Don't you think this is a little ridiculous? I already came out of your apartment a few minutes ago."

"But nobody noticed."

"They noticed," he grumbled. "And what was that about my wife?"

"I told them she ran off."

"Why?"

"Postpartum depression." Daisy shrugged. "It was all I could think of. They caught me by surprise."

"No, I meant why did you tell them I was married?"

"You didn't want them gossiping. So I decided to go for the pity factor." She smiled, looking ridiculously appealing even though her yellow topknot was listing to the left and a strand of blond hair trailed down her neck. It wasn't a good time to picture her naked and in his bed, but Will couldn't stop the fleeting image that flashed through his mind.

"But did you have to tell them I was married?"

She shrugged. "Is that so bad?"

"Honey," he said, surprising himself by bending over to whisper in her pretty little ear. "It's a fate worse than death."

5

"I DON'T UNDERSTAND MEN."

"Of course not," Barlow said. "No matter what my wife says, we're complicated creatures." He dipped a long-handled spoon into the soup pot and tasted tomorrow's special, Texas chili, then made a face of disgust.

"How is it?" Daisy stopped fiddling with her pencil. She was tired of adding columns and wondering if she was making enough money. "Ready for the contest?"

He tossed the spoon in the sink. "Not hot enough."

"That's what you always say, and then I spend two hours refilling water glasses." Daisy peeked through the large rectangular opening to make sure no new customers walked in. "From now on I'm going to mind my own business, especially when it comes to taking care of babies."

"Good luck."

"You don't think I can?"

He opened the cooler and stored the pot of chili inside. "You're living in a small town now, Daize. There's no such thing as privacy."

"That's what Will Wilson said."

"He should know." Barlow took his black leather jacket off the hook by the door. "Everyone in town will be talking about him and that baby, you wait and see."

"I guess I shouldn't have told Mrs. Murphy and Maude Anderson that Will's wife ran off."

"He's married?"

"No. I made that up. I don't know what came over me." All of a sudden she'd felt so darned protective of both the man and the baby. It seemed ridiculous now, when she had time to think. When she had time to think of other things to say, like...nothing at all. Her mother had always told her to think before she spoke, yet that was something she hadn't learned. Until now.

Barlow grinned and put on his jacket. "And you think *men* are hard to understand?"

"I guess it was that darling baby." Her sweet face and those trusting blue eyes had melted Daisy's heart.

"Uh-oh."

"What?"

"Whenever Bonnie gets that look on her face, we end up rescuing another dog."

"How many do you have?"

"Five." He sighed. "You know how much dog food costs?"

Daisy didn't think he really wanted an answer. "I'm not going to start adopting kids. I have enough trouble now. Do you think I need to raise the price of a bowl of chili?"

"You need to get some rest, hire some evening help. If you're not careful, you're going to burn out."

"When Darlene comes in, I'll go lie down for a while."

"Promise?"

"Sure." Darlene, a widow who worked in the high-school cafeteria, liked picking up extra hours at the café during the week. "She knows that grill almost as well as you do."

"There's plenty of roast beef sliced for open-faced sandwiches and the gravy is on the stove. Don't forget to stir it once in a while. See you tomorrow."

"Thanks."

"And stay away from that baby or the next thing I know you'll be telling me you're pregnant," he warned.

"Not a chance," she quipped, thinking at the same time how wonderful that might be. If she had a husband. If she had a husband who would actually stick around long enough to be a father. Barlow left out the side door. A blustery wind fanned her legs before the door closed behind him. It looked like it was going to be another horribly cold night. Would Spring be safe and warm? Would that cowboy take care of her properly?

"I will mind my own business," she repeated once again. "Even if three hundred homeless babies start screaming right in the middle of the supper rush." She returned to her account book and tried not to think of Spring.

"THAT'S IT?"

Joe tossed the file onto the pile of papers in the middle of his desk. "That's all I can do right now, unless you have some idea where she'd be."

Will leaned back in his chair and rubbed his eyes. "If I did I would have gone there already. The last time I heard she was living in Salmon, Idaho, but when I got there she was gone and no one knew where."

"No letters, phone calls?"

"A postcard from Boise about two years ago, after the funeral. I kept hoping she'd come back after that."

"But she didn't." Joe leaned back and studied his friend. "You look like hell."

"Yeah. I'm worried about her and what's happened. And I'm sure praying she comes back soon for her daughter." He glanced down at his feet at the baby asleep in her car seat. She was asleep at last, having survived a trip out to the ranch to check on the animals. He'd managed to do his chores in record time while Spring had slept inside the barn. Thank goodness he didn't have to do much more than feed the horses and let them out. Bozeman was content with a full dish of dog food and fresh water, but otherwise preferred to go in and out through a door Will had cut in the porch. He'd been sleeping in the middle of Will's unmade bed, too, most likely happy to have the place to himself.

"You might want to buy an answering machine,

just in case anyone calls. And I'll let you know if anything turns up."

"All right."

"Go talk to Jane. She's dying to see that baby and she said she'd make a list of baby-sitters for you."

"Thanks. I guess I can't sleep at Daisy's place again."

Joe grinned. "You should have seen her face when she saw you in her bed. I don't think she was real pleased."

"If I was a little younger and a lot less tired..." He would charm the apron off the lovely waitress.

"Dream on, pal. Every single man in town has been trying to work up the courage to ask her out."

"Has she really been married twice?" If that was true, were there two men in this world who were that stupid?

"I guess."

"Wonder what went wrong."

"You'd better ask her that."

"Right. And get ready to duck. I don't think Ms. McGregor answers personal questions." Spring fussed and opened her eyes, so Will reached down and plucked her from the car seat. "Did you hear how I got married and my wife left me? Daisy told Hazel Murphy, so it's all over town now."

Joe chuckled. "Jane called and wanted to know if it was true."

Will swore under his breath.

"You and Daisy make quite a pair," Joe pointed out. "And she saved your ass last night."

"I left most of my stuff there. I guess I'd better go pick it up."

Joe ignored his ringing phone. "That ranch house is no place for a little baby, Will."

"I put in a new furnace."

"But you haven't had time to insulate. Little babies can't be in drafty places. They get sick." Joe leaned forward. "I can get her placed in a temporary foster home, where she'll be taken care of until we find Sarah—or whoever her mother is. I'm not convinced that someone isn't playing a joke on you."

"Some joke," he said, looking down at Spring's tiny, trusting face.

"Or this could be someone who really thinks you are the father. We know Sarah's blood type from her medical records when she was a kid. A simple blood test on Spring could give us more info to go on, or even rule out Sarah as the mother."

"I know. You've said that before."

"And?"

"Not yet." He put the baby up to his shoulder and snuggled her against his cheek. She smelled like powder and sour milk. "This baby stays with me. Besides, I'd like to act like a daddy for a while longer." He paused, then added, "As long as it's temporary."

HE'D PICK UP the baby's stuff at Daisy's and then he'd go home. Boy, was that a grim prospect. There were drafts and dog hair and not-so-clean floors, not the kind of home a baby should have.

But then none of this was what a baby should have, Will thought. And he figured that little Spring knew it, too, because she'd started to scream the minute they left the sheriff's office. She'd screamed in the truck, even though he'd driven around town a few times because an hour ago she'd liked to ride in the truck and he'd figured he'd found the solution to all his problems: feed her, burp her, then drive her around.

He glanced over at her red face. So much for that solution. She might be hungry or she might be wet, and neither one could be fixed right this second. And his truck suddenly smelled like the baby had done more than just pee.

This was obviously a job for a woman. He executed a neat U-turn in the middle of Main Street and headed back the way he came.

None of the teenagers goofing around in the booths looked up as he entered the café with Spring screaming in his arms, but Daisy stopped whatever she was doing with a calculator and a pad of paper to frown at him as he walked across the room.

"What have you done to her?"

"Nothing. She's female." He deposited the baby into Daisy's outstretched arms. Boy, was he grateful for those arms. "She enjoys yelling at me."

"Someone needs her diaper changed."

"I would have done it," he lied, "but all her stuff is here."

"You didn't take a diaper bag with you?"

"What's a diaper bag?"

"It's what mothers carry around with them. It has diapers and bottles and all sorts of things a baby needs. You have to take it with you wherever you go."

"There ought to be a book about this stuff."

"There is. I mean, there are. Go to the library and start reading." She stood up.

"Now?"

Her withering look would have unmanned a lesser cowboy. "Pick up my stuff, will you? We're going to give you a poopy-diaper lesson."

Not exactly the stuff of fantasies. "Can I get a beer first?"

"We both will," she promised. "I'll meet you at the other door." She paused at the counter. "Darlene, I'll be in the back if you need me."

Will stopped and peered through the kitchen opening. "Hey, Darlene. I haven't seen you since high school."

The tall brunette waved a spatula at him and grinned. "Hey, Billy! I heard you were back home again."

"I'll be back for one of those burgers," he promised, hurrying outside into the cold wind. He really wished Daisy would let him go through the back way. It wasn't as if she was fooling anyone. It wasn't as if they were having sex in the storage room.

Which he wouldn't mind, come to think of it. The woman was gorgeous, but there was something else he couldn't put his finger on. Mysterious, maybe. Though he'd never been around mysterious women before. His experience was limited to "Hey, hon, can I buy you a beer?"

He put his head down against the wind and rounded the corner. He'd forgotten how hard the wind could blow in the middle of January. Daisy opened the door before he knocked, and he hurried into the tiny kitchen.

"Feels like snow again." He shivered.

"I didn't expect to see you this afternoon. I thought you'd gone home," she said.

"I did, long enough to check on the horses and feed my dog."

She handed him the promised bottle of beer. "Why did you come back to town?"

"I don't think I can do this by myself," he admitted, taking a swallow.

"Of course you can't. You'd have to be crazy to even try."

He tried to smile. "I've had worse things than crazy said about me."

"This is different." She nodded toward the baby in her arms. "This is her life we're talking about. Do you have any family—mother, sisters, aunts, grandparents—anyone who could help you out for a while? Until you find Spring's mother?"

"Not even close."

"What about Sarah? Do you know if she has a family you could contact?"

"Joe's working on that." He didn't blame her for

wondering. She thought he was the kind of man who left unwed mothers to fend for themselves. "And if I told you she wasn't my daughter, would you believe me?"

Daisy handed him the baby, but didn't meet his gaze. "Not really. Why would you go to all this trouble for a child who wasn't yours?"

"Because..." he began, following her into the living room. He watched as she gathered up an armful of baby things.

"It's none of my business," she said, taking a deep breath. "But obviously you don't believe in practicing safe sex. I mean, doesn't anyone watch television, for heaven's sake?"

"Television?"

"You're supposed to use condoms, cowboy." She motioned towards the baby. "Bring her into the bathroom and we'll do it on the counter."

"We?" He gulped.

"You have to learn sometime."

"I could wait," he suggested, noticing that Spring had a definite ripe odor to her. "I could wait a long time," Will said, following Daisy into the bathroom.

"I'M MISSING OUT on all the fun."

"What?"

"The fun," Jane repeated, wondering why her husband didn't understand what she was saying. "The mystery baby. Will acting like a father. Daisy McGregor acting maternal." She fidgeted in the recliner and surveyed her large stomach. "All this exciting stuff is happening while I sit here like a lump. A big fat baby-making lump."

"I'll tell Will to stop by with the baby soon, okay?"

"Like he's going to tell me anything."

"What do you want to know?"

Men were idiots. Even her sweet, perplexed deputy-sheriff husband. "I want to know if Will likes Daisy, if Daisy likes Will. I want to know if she's good enough for him. I want to see that poor little baby. I want to know who left her on Will's doorstep." Her voice rose and Joe moved back a step. "Give me something to do. I could make phone calls. Track down clues. Talk to hospitals," she pleaded. "At least I'd feel involved."

"You did something. You lent him the bassinet," he offered, stepping over a miniature yellow dump truck. "Where are the boys?"

"They're having a 'quiet time' in their room for a while." The baby kicked her again and Jane patted her stomach. "Your daughter, on the other hand, is doing somersaults in here."

Joe came closer and put one hand on her stomach. "Yeah, I can feel her. Long day, huh?"

She sighed and folded her hands over his. "A very long day. I can barely move."

"You see the doctor tomorrow?"

"Yes. He'll say what he always says: that baby will be born when it's good and ready." She looked up at her husband and cursed the tears that welled in her eyes. "I really wish this baby was ready now."

"Oh, honey," Joe drawled, leaning over to kiss her cheek. "What do you want me to do?"

"Take me out to dinner," she said. "I need some fresh air."

"The windchill's thirteen below."

"Walking's good for starting labor."

Joe straightened. "I'll bundle up the boys good and warm."

"Will you find out where Will is? Maybe he'd like to join us?"

"So you could see that baby."

She sniffed, then smiled at herself for being so silly. "You have to admit that it must be a pretty strange sight."

"Will with a baby? Yeah," he said. "He's doing okay, though."

"I meant Daisy McGregor. She doesn't look like the motherly type." She held out her hand so Joe could help her to her feet. It took a couple of humiliating minutes to get to a vertical position. "This is my last pregnancy."

"You said that last time."

"I mean it. I used to have a figure like Daisy's." She paused, thinking of the waitress's ample bosom and tiny waist. "Well, not exactly. But I wouldn't mind seeing my feet again. One of the school mothers thinks Daisy used to be Miss Utah in the Miss America pageant. Do you think Daisy is her real name?"

"I wouldn't know."

"Sure you would. You know everything."

"Not that," he said, calling for the boys.

"I just don't get it."

"Get what?" he called over the excited voices of their sons.

"How on earth could a woman like Daisy McGregor know anything about babies?"

THE SUPPER RUSH WASN'T.

"We've got burgers, hot dogs, chili or hot roast-beef sandwiches," Daisy told the Pierce family, who were one of two groups of customers at five-thirty. "Fries, pies and chocolate cake. Ice cream, Jell-O with whipped cream. Potato chips, pickles, ham salad and baked beans. Next week we're going to have pizza every night, too."

"Cool," the older boy said. "I'm gonna have Jell-O and beans." He noticed his father's frown and added, "Please."

"Me, too," the smaller child said, grinning from ear to ear. Both boys were miniature versions of their father, with dark eyes and hair.

Daisy didn't write the order on her pad. Instead she looked at Jane, who appeared awkward and uncomfortable in the booth.

"That's okay," their mother said, waving off Joe's objections. "Beans are protein and they can have milk with their supper." She closed the menu. "I'd like a piece of chocolate cake with vanilla ice cream on top."

Her husband stared. "For dinner?"

"It's a craving," she informed him, before smiling at Daisy. "I've been pregnant for a hundred months now and I think I'm entitled."

Daisy wrote down the order and then asked, "The baby's due soon?"

"Any day now. Or I'm going to explode."

"She always gets a little strange at the end," Joe explained. "I'll have the hot roast-beef sandwich and an order of fries. And coffee, too."

"Sure. Would you like anything to drink?" she asked the pregnant woman.

"A cup of tea would be perfect," the pretty brunette said. "You haven't officially met my boys. The older one is Josh and the younger is Jimmy."

"Hi, guys," Daisy said. "I'm glad you came to have supper here."

"They're thrilled to be out of the house," Jane said, "and so am I. Have you seen Will anywhere around?"

"He's in back with the baby." She'd left him rocking Spring while watching a rodeo on one of the satellite channels. The baby almost looked as if she was enjoying herself.

"I'm dying to see her."

"Want me to tell him you're here?"

"You can give him this." Jane pulled out a piece of paper from her pocket and handed it to Daisy. "He asked for names of baby-sitters, but I think he needs a lot more help than that. Have you ever seen that house he's living in?"

"No, but I'll tell him you're—"

"It has possibilities, if you're willing to spend a ton of money and a whole lot of time restoring it to its original condition, it would be gorgeous. Like one of those places you'd see in a home-remodeling magazine."

Joe reached into his pocket. "There goes the beeper," he groaned, and his family joined him. He glanced at the number and winced. "Looks like I need to make a phone call. Can I use your phone, Daisy?"

"Sure. It's behind the counter, next to the cash register."

The older boy slid out of the booth to let his father leave. "What kind of Jell-O do you have?"

"Orange," Daisy told him. "And I'll bet you want whipped cream on it, too."

"Yes. Please."

"Darn." Jane snuggled the smaller son close to her. "Here we thought we were going to have dinner with Dad."

"I'll be right back with your drinks," Daisy promised, squashing a pang of envy as she hurried to the counter to place their order. She hoped Jane Pierce knew how lucky she was.

"Daisy." Joe intercepted her before she could return with the drinks. "Can I go back and get Will?"

"Something's wrong."

His grim expression didn't change. "I'm not sure. I think we may have found the woman we've been looking for."

"TWO WOMEN and three kids," Jane said, looking across the booth at Daisy. "What did we do to deserve this?"

She laughed. "Just a couple of hours ago I'd told myself I was going to mind my own business." Now she had a sleeping baby in her arms and a sticky-faced and cheerful five-year-old beside her.

"What fun is that?" Jane scooped another mound of ice cream from the dish. "I promised myself I wouldn't gain any more than twenty pounds this time around, that I would eat salads and fresh fruits every day."

"A noble goal," Daisy agreed. "But ice cream tastes better."

"True. And eating helps pass the time." Jane pointed the spoon toward Spring. "That is one beautiful baby."

"Do you think they'll find her mother?"

Jane sighed. "Do you want them to?"

"You have to admit, anyone who would leave her baby on someone's doorstep in the middle of January doesn't exactly qualify for Mother of the Year."

"Sit still, Jimmy. Eat your beans." She turned her attention back to Daisy. "I know."

"And if she was alone..."

"Without a husband, you mean?"

"Without anyone, but especially without Will. He shares responsibility in this."

Jane moved the empty ice-cream dish out of her way and picked up her teacup. "You're assuming Will's the father."

Josh tugged on Daisy's sleeve. "My daddy's a sheriff."

She smiled down at him. "I know."

"He's got a fast car."

"I'll bet he does," Daisy said, turning back to the boy's mother. "Why shouldn't I? Assume he's the father, I mean. The baby was left on his ranch and he's taking care of her instead of putting her in a foster home until Joe can find the mother."

Jane shrugged. "All I'm saying is that I wouldn't jump to conclusions if I were you."

"It doesn't matter. It's none of my business," Daisy repeated, reminding herself once again. "It really isn't."

"Except that you're sitting here holding someone else's baby." Jane put her hand on her belly and leaned against the back of the booth. "Is it true you were in the Miss America pageant? The whole town wants to know."

"You can spread the word that I was third runner-up for Miss Wyoming. The talent contest killed me."

Jane laughed. "What did you do?"

"Oh, no, you don't," she said, shaking her head. "I'd have to know you a lot better or I'd have to be drinking frozen margaritas."

"What's that?" Jimmy asked. "Your baby's gettin' mad."

Daisy looked down to see Spring about to yell. She fussed and wriggled as if the world was completely out of kilter. "She sure is. I'll bet she needs her bottle."

Josh lifted his head from his mother's side. "A bottle?"

"Bottles are for babies," Jane assured him. "See that little baby there? We're going to have one of those soon." She patted her rounded belly. "Very soon, I hope."

"I'd better go take care of this little girl before she starts to scream."

"Let Daisy out of the booth, Josh. I guess we'd better get home, too."

"Joe said he'd call when they got to town?"

She nodded. "He promised."

"Stay here, then. The kids can watch television in the back. I just have to help Darlene close up." She looked around the room. "We don't get much of a crowd at night. Everyone tells me that January, February and March are the slowest months of the year here in town."

"Selling pizza is a good idea. Can people order it to go?"

"Sure. I bought a used pizza oven in North Bend. And we're having the chili cook-off here on Wednesday night."

"That's the fund-raiser for the high-school basketball team, right?" Jane eased Josh out of the booth and began to clear the table.

"Stop that," Daisy said. "You're not supposed to be working."

Jane ignored her and motioned to her sons to help. "Moving around could start labor."

"Not tonight, please?" Daisy couldn't help laughing. "I think one baby is enough for now."

"Easy for you to say," Jane grumbled, but she didn't look upset. "Let's see what happens when you're three days overdue."

Daisy patted Josh's dark curls. "I would love that, I really would."

"You're not thinking that Will—"

"Oh, no," she assured the worried woman. "I'm looking for a family man, one who wants to settle down. I've had enough wild cowboys to last me a lifetime."

Jane grinned. "Let's finish up here so you can tell me all about them."

"There's not much—"

"Sure there is," Jane said, carrying an armload of dirty plates across the room. "You forget that a pregnant woman is easily entertained."

"Okay, but don't forget I warned you." Daisy hurried after her with the baby. "You take Spring and I'll take care of the dishes." It had been a long time since she'd had a friend.

It felt good. At least she could thank Will Wilson for that.

6

"NO PROBLEM." Joe hung up the radio in his Explorer and stepped on the gas. "Jane and the kids are at Daisy's. I'll pick them up there."

"Good." Will watched the miles of prairie speed by in the darkness. "What a mess, huh?"

"Yeah."

"What if I can't find her?" He felt Joe's gaze on him, but he kept looking out the side window.

"We'll find her. Someone will turn up sooner or later, whether it's Sarah or somebody else," his friend assured him. "All in all, I think you're pretty lucky."

"Yeah?" He turned toward him. "How's that?"

"You haven't had any relatives around here for a long time. If this baby is Sarah's, then you've got a family again." The radio squawked and Joe raised the volume to listen to an exchange between a deputy and the dispatcher. A truck was in a ditch on the north side of town.

Family. Will smiled to himself as the meager lights of Cowman's Corner shone in the distance. "I'm not sure I'd call me and that little baby a family."

"It's about time," Joe declared. "Don't you ever think about settling down?"

Well, damn it, he wasn't sure he wanted to think about that question, so he and Joe spent the last five miles listening to the dispatcher chat about the weather and the latest score of the high school basketball game. Joe drove around to the back of the café and parked along the sidewalk next to Daisy's private entrance. Light spilled over the door and through the curtained windows. Joe shut off the engine and opened the door. "Well, should we go check on our kids?"

"Shut up," Will said, taking a deep breath as he opened the door and stepped out into the cold night. He'd become a family man after two days? No way. He was protecting his own, that was all. He followed Joe to the door and waited for Daisy to open it and let them inside where it would be warm.

"Hi," she said, looking up into their faces, wondering if there was good news. "Come on in. The boys fell asleep watching TV, and Jane and I were having tea. Did you find—who you were looking for?"

"No. Not yet." Joe took off his hat and wiped his feet on the mat. "Is Jane doing okay?"

"She's fine. We've had fun."

Joe hurried into the living room, but Will paused in front of Daisy. She didn't look like herself, but he couldn't figure out what was different. That curly hair was loose and wild and she'd changed into jeans and a faded yellow sweatshirt, but that wasn't the change. She looked happy. Will inhaled the scent of apple pie. "Something smells good."

"I took a pie out of the freezer. We got hungry." She touched his sleeve. "I'm sorry about tonight."

"Yeah. She turned out to be someone else, a woman running away from her husband. The baby turned up at her sister's house."

"Come on in and get warm." She dropped her hand from his arm and he followed Joe into the living room, where two little boys lay sprawled in a heap of blankets on the floor. "Spring's asleep in the bedroom. I fed her and she fell asleep right away."

"We've had a good time," Jane said, stretched out on the couch. "Daisy's been waiting on me too much, though."

Will wasn't surprised. "She likes to take care of people."

Daisy paused in the doorway. "Would you two like pie and coffee, or would you rather have a sandwich? There's roast beef out front."

"God, that sounds good." Joe sat down by his wife's stocking feet and took them on his lap. "You look okay," he said, worry lines easing from his face.

"Quit worrying," Janie said. "We've been having fun."

Will turned from the domestic scene of sleeping children and a loving couple to look at Daisy. Big mistake. Despite the beauty-queen looks, she was definitely the kind of woman who wanted a home and family and a man to rub her feet at the end of the day. He could tell from the wistful expression in her eyes as she looked at the Pierces. "Is the beef in the restaurant?"

"Yes. In the cooler."

"I can go through the back and get it? I wouldn't want you to get mad at me again."

"I'll make the sandwiches there," she said. "It'll be easier."

He didn't ask her if she wanted help, because he knew she'd most likely refuse. So he followed her through the hall and waited while she turned the key in the lock. She turned to look back at him. "What are you doing?"

"Being with you."

"Well, don't," she muttered, opening the door to the back room.

"Why not?" He lengthened his strides to keep up with her as she hurried into the dimly lit restaurant.

She ignored the question. Instead she went behind the counter and disappeared into the kitchen, leaving Will no choice but to follow.

"Mustard or mayonnaise?" she asked, opening the cooler and retrieving a packet he assumed was the meat.

"Mayo." He stepped closer as she took a jar of mayonnaise and set it on the counter. "What's going on?"

"Wheat or white?" She grabbed two loaves of bread on a shelf by the freezer.

"Come on, Daisy." He put his hand on her arm. Gently, so not to scare her. "What's the matter?"

She took a deep shuddering breath and that was

when he realized she was crying. He saw a tear hit the spotless metal counter. "Go somewhere else."

"No way." One thing he understood was a weeping woman. Lord knew he'd dealt with his share. "Come here," he whispered, folding her neatly into his arms. She resisted at first, but a couple of tugs had her against his chest. He could feel her trying to get control of herself, but she didn't pull out of his arms. She was a little thing, with the top of her head barely up to his chin. He tried to ignore the feeling of those incredible breasts touching his shirt, tried to concentrate on Daisy's mysterious tears. He held her in his arms for too short a time, because he wasn't ready to let her go when she finally pulled away.

"Sorry," she said, reaching for the paper towels. She wiped her face and gave him a funny lopsided smile. "It just came over me."

He remembered that look of longing when she'd thought no one noticed. "What is it that you want and you don't have?"

"Nothing." She took a deep breath. "Wheat or white for your sandwich?"

"Do you miss your husband?" He wondered if the poor bastard knew what kind of a woman he'd left.

"Please stop." Her voice was low as she turned away and fiddled with the metal tie that sealed the bag. "Just let me do this. You must be starving, and I—"

He put his hands on her shoulders and turned her

around. "Daisy, would you quit for a minute?" Before he realized what he was doing, he bent and touched his lips to hers. She was sweet and warm, her lips soft and slightly parted against his. She melted against him for a brief moment, just long enough to tempt him to lengthen the kiss. Long enough to feel like he'd been tossed into the air by a three-thousand-pound bull.

And long enough to make him want to haul her into his arms and carry her to bed. And if ever there was a woman who looked ready for bed, it was Daisy. He didn't know which one of them stopped the kiss, but when she backed away and he looked down at her, that was his first thought. Bed. Or better yet, the kitchen counter.

Daisy looked up at him as if she was going to start crying again. "Aw, honey," he said, moving to hold her again.

She glared at him and took a step backward. "Don't you 'honey' me."

"Why not? You kissed me back."

"Well, of course I did. But I'm not going to do it again, so go away."

"Are you sure?" He watched as she selected a particularly sharp knife from the rack above the chopping board. "Yeah, I guess you are."

"I am through with cowboys," she muttered.

"Let me take a wild guess here," he drawled, reaching past her for the mayonnaise jar. He opened it and set it on the counter. "Was your ex-husband a cowboy?"

"Yes," she said, her back to him as she assembled thick sandwiches. "Both of them."

"Both?" He gulped, yet it wasn't surprising that a woman who looked like Daisy McGregor had had men lined up to marry her. "What happened to, uh, them?"

"They're both still alive, if that's what you're wondering." She cut the sandwiches into thick wedges and put them on plates. She added pickles and potato chips, then picked up both plates and turned around. "I didn't poison their chili or stab them while they were sleeping. Here."

He took one of the plates. "Looks good. Thanks."

"You're welcome," she said, leading him out of the kitchen. He lengthened his strides to keep up with her.

"Neither of them rubbed your feet, huh?"

Before Daisy slipped through the door to her apartment, she stopped and looked up at him. "Both of them turned out to like rubbing other women's feet," she said. "Which is one of the reasons why I'm not going to let myself get involved with another sweet-talking cowboy who can't keep his jeans zipped."

"Meaning me."

Daisy sighed. "Especially you, Will. You're not even married and you have a baby you didn't even know about two days ago and somewhere out there is that baby's mother and I won't even start telling you what I think of her for what she's done." She took a deep breath and looked him right in the eye.

"I'm looking for a man who wants to settle down and have kids and go to Parents' Night at school, not some rodeo star who hasn't figured out safe sex and birth control."

Will didn't speak until she had spun around and started to walk away. "So I guess that means I'm not spending the night?"

She didn't answer, so he figured she'd lost her sense of humor. Truth was, he should have told her all about Sarah, but damn, he didn't like explaining himself. And he didn't owe anyone here in Cowman's Corner a damn thing.

"AND THEN WHAT happened?" Barlow cracked four eggs onto the grill and wiped his hands on the towel wrapped around his waist.

"He ate his sandwich and went home. Everybody went home," she added, remembering how gentle Joe Pierce had been with his sleeping boys. "Except the baby. She stayed with me." She didn't tell Barlow that she'd enjoyed the company, or that she'd rocked the baby until they'd both fallen asleep in the chair. Spring didn't seem to mind that Daisy couldn't carry a tune. Daisy glanced over at the baby, who was wide awake and snug in her car seat at Daisy's feet. "You're such a good girl," she told her, and the child waved her arms.

"And that was okay with Billy?"

"Will," she corrected, going back to writing a list of supplies she needed to get in North Bend. "He didn't have a choice, really. I guess that house is no place for a baby."

"That's where he was raised, I think," Barlow said. "His grandmother left him the ranch when she died a while back. Everyone in town thought he'd just put it up for sale."

"Why?"

"They were an odd group out there. His mother moved back in with her parents after her youngest was born and I guess it wasn't one big happy family. We're gonna need extra onions," he said.

She underlined the *onions*. "He said something about selling it. After he fixes it up."

"That's going to take some money, I'll bet." He walked past her carrying a plate piled high with eggs and hash browns. "Darlene! Your order's up!"

"Okay," she called from the other side of the pass-through. "You don't have to yell."

"Yes, I do," Barlow said, "or Gordon's going to be complaining about cold eggs again."

Spring screeched and kicked her feet, so Daisy leaned over and tickled her chin. "You like all the noise, sweetheart? When you get older your daddy can bring you in here and you can have all the ice cream you want, okay?"

"When is Daddy coming to get her?"

Daisy looked at her watch and then leaned over to play peekaboo with Spring. She loved the way the baby's blue eyes widened with surprise each time. "Peekaboo! I see you! He'll be here any time now. I told him to come before eight."

"Good thing Darlene's working with Heather today," Barlow said. "You're a little distracted."

"What?" She straightened and picked up her pen. "What do you want radishes for?"

Barlow sighed and went back to his grill. "Never mind, Daize. You did the right thing."

"I hope so. Even used, this pizza oven wasn't cheap."

"I meant, sending Billy Wilson home last night. He's not your type."

"I know. I thought about it a lot last night." She wrote family man at the bottom of her list. "Maybe I'll tell Leroy Doyle I'll go out with him the next time he asks me."

"He's sure asked you enough times," Barlow muttered. "But jeez, Daisy, Leroy Doyle?"

"Orders!" Heather called, pinning three slips to the clipboard. "We just got a rush."

"You need help?"

"Nah, I can handle it." Heather grinned. "How's the baby doing?"

"She's fine. Happy."

"What are you saying about Leroy? Did he ask you out again?"

Daisy shrugged. "I thought I might start dating, that's all."

"But he has kids," Heather protested. "Three of them."

"That's okay."

"But they're teenagers, Daisy. Can't you find a guy with no kids?"

"I like kids."

"Obviously." She turned when the door jangled. "Your boyfriend just walked in."

"Who?"

Heather gave her a thumbs-up sign. "He looks like he needs coffee," she said, and disappeared from Daisy's view. She assumed the thumbs-up meant that Will was here to pick up his daughter, which was good. She had a lot to do today and the sooner she started the better.

"I guess we'd better go see your daddy," she told Spring, bending to unhook the safety strap that held the baby in the seat. She lifted her into her arms and grabbed the top of the car seat with her free hand. It was time to stop playing mommy and start acting like someone who had a business to run. She would treat Will like any other customer, like any other person who needed help. She'd made herself perfectly clear last night, she told herself, stepping into the restaurant and seeing Will cross the room toward them. He was smiling, damn him. A honey-I-could-eat-you-up smile that was designed to make a woman believe anything he said.

But he wasn't looking at Daisy.

"How's my girl?" He held out his arms and Daisy put the baby into them.

"She's fine. I think she likes the smell of food."

"Yeah, she's a Wilson, all right." He looked past her shoulder. "Good. An empty booth. I can grab some breakfast before I head out."

"Here's the seat."

He took it and headed across the room, with Daisy hurrying behind him. "Did she keep you up all night?"

"No." She almost wished he'd shown up a little later. She wasn't ready to stop playing mom. "She woke up at two for her bottle, but she went right back to sleep. She ate at six—"

"Meaning you were late for work?"

"I have Heather filling in for me today, so it didn't matter." She hovered like an anxious auntie, suddenly unwilling to leave Spring in her daddy's care. He managed to get the baby settled in her car seat beside him, then looked up at Daisy again.

"You have the day off?"

Before Daisy could reply, Heather appeared and set a coffee cup in front of him and filled it from the glass carafe. "Daisy's going to North Bend today, for the pizza oven."

"Great," he said, checking to make sure Spring was safely tucked into the corner. "That's where we're going, too."

"Cool." Heather took the order pad from her pocket. "You want breakfast first?"

"Sure do." He turned that dazzling smile toward the young waitress. "Just give me a couple of fried eggs and some bacon. Throw some toast on the plate, too."

"Will do." She grinned at Daisy. "I'll bet Billy could help you with the oven."

"I don't—"

"Good idea." Will leaned forward, ignoring his

coffee and looking like he was going to touch her hand. She quickly put her hands in her lap and then felt like an idiot. "I'll buy you lunch," he continued, "if you'll join us."

"Us?"

"Me and Spring. We're going to buy a crib for her new room."

"I didn't think your house—" She stopped, reluctant to hurt his feelings by repeating what Jane had said about the building not being suitable for an infant.

"Was fit for a kid?"

"Well..."

"I'm working on it." He took a swallow of coffee and Daisy noticed the dark shadows under his eyes. He hadn't shaved, either, which should have made him look sinister, but only added to all that masculine sex appeal.

She refused to fall for it. After all, she didn't have time to sit around staring at handsome cowboys all day.

"I've been insulating windows," he explained. "I'm getting rid of the drafts. Downstairs, anyway, so Spring won't catch cold."

"Then you don't think her mother's coming back."

"I hope she will," he said, glancing toward the content baby. "I'm scared to death of all this." His gaze met Daisy's, and she was surprised at the naked honesty there. "Just give me a few more hours,

Daisy. And then I promise we won't bother you again."

She should have said no. She should have slipped out of the booth, grabbed her shopping list and hustled to her car. "Okay. And you're not bothering me," she heard herself say. *Liar.*

"Thanks, Daisy." He smiled.

She really wished he wouldn't.

"THERE ARE TIMES when I really hate being married to a cop."

Joe refilled her coffee cup without asking his wife if she wanted more. "Yeah?" He kissed the top of her head before he sat down at the table for his mid-morning coffee break. Jane knew darn well he was there to check on her, see if she was having contractions. It was aggravating to have absolutely nothing happening at all. "Why is that?"

"Because you never tell me anything. Like who Spring's mother is and why Will has the baby."

"Can't," he said, pulling a plate of cookies closer. "Classified information. Where'd you get these?"

"From the freezer," she said, watching him eat two. The man would never gain weight, not even if he ate fifty sugar cookies a day. "I baked them months ago. When I had a waist." She patted her round belly, covered by her largest maternity blouse. "Our daughter is in no hurry to be born."

"Neither were the boys," he reminded her, taking a bite out of his fourth cookie.

It wouldn't be fair to Daisy if she fell in love with

Will and then Will's old girlfriend returned. "I like her."

"Who?"

"Daisy McGregor."

"The woman makes one heck of a roast beef sandwich."

"She's perfect for Will."

"No one's perfect for Will."

"She's just what he needs."

Her husband's eyebrows rose. "You're matchmaking? For Will?" He began to laugh, which Jane decided was a sign of a man who'd had too much sugar, so she moved the cookie plate away. "Save some for the kids. They'll be home from school in an hour."

"Will's got enough problems right now. He sure doesn't need a girlfriend."

"Whose the mother of that baby and where is she?"

He shook his head. "You know I can't discuss police business."

"Since when?"

"Honey, I don't have much to tell, that's all. Why so interested?"

"Because I don't want that woman showing up, wrecking everything."

"Let me take a guess here. 'That woman' is Spring's mother and 'wrecking everything' means your matchmaking schemes for Will?"

"Exactly."

"Sweetheart, Will needs a baby-sitter for that

baby. And he could use a construction crew, if he still plans to sell that place of his. And he needs to find Spring's mother." This time he didn't look like he was teasing her. "And it's my job to help him do it." He stood up and brushed crumbs from his pants. "I wouldn't worry about whether he has a date on a Saturday night."

"And what about Daisy?" Jane had seen the wistful expression on her new friend's face when she'd taken care of that baby. If ever there was a woman who wanted a family, it was Daisy McGregor.

"I've got to get back to work," Joe said, taking his jacket from the back of the chair. He bent down and kissed his wife before adding, "I wouldn't worry too much about Daisy if I were you. That's one lady who can take care of herself."

Which of course only proved that men didn't know anything at all about women. Jane waited until she heard the truck roar out of the drive before she reached for the phone.

7

HIS VOW TO LEAVE Daisy alone hadn't lasted long. Just five minutes after seeing her again, in fact. He hadn't intended to ask her to go with him to town, but he hadn't wanted to leave her, either. Because of Spring, he reminded himself. Nothing more. Fingers fumbling with seat belt straps, Will attached the baby's car seat in the narrow back seat of the truck, then stepped out of the way to let Daisy climb into the passenger seat.

Once they were all settled, Will started the engine and headed out of town. Daisy hadn't said a word for over ten minutes, a situation that Will was determined to change. "You know," he began, stepping on the gas as they reached the ramp to the interstate. "Just because of last night doesn't mean you can't talk to me."

She looked up from the paper she was studying and stared at him. "What?"

"Last night. Kissing you. I apologized."

"Oh," she said. "That."

His ego evaporated into the cold Montana air. Will reached over and turned the heater up.

"I wasn't ignoring you on purpose." Daisy folded up her paper and tucked it into the pocket of her coat. "I was trying to figure out how to make the most of my time so I wouldn't be gone too long. The chili contest is tomorrow night and I need to be prepared."

"Oh." He wished she wasn't so damned gorgeous. That long golden suede coat she wore made her look even more like the beauty queen she was rumored to be. He kept his hands gripping the steering wheel and managed to stay on the road. "Nice day out."

"Yes."

"The roads are fairly clear."

She obliging looked out the window. "Yes, they are."

"You're not mad because of last night, are you?"

Daisy shrugged. "I'm a big girl, Will. That kind of thing doesn't bother me."

Which was even worse, as far as he was concerned, since "that kind of thing" had kept him awake most of the night, which he'd spent caulking the openings around the first-floor windows. He hadn't even needed to make a pot of coffee. All he'd had to do was think about how Daisy's lips tasted of sugar and apples and he'd been edgy enough to wash the damn windows once he'd winterized them. The living room smelled like vinegar, the way it used to when his mother was alive.

His mother had fought against dust and dirt all of her life, always struggling to meet the demands of Hank and Edna. "Do you have family around here?" he heard himself ask.

"No. I'm from Nevada. Most of the family is still there, outside of Reno. I go back once in a while. What about you?"

"My mother's parents left me the ranch," he said, not turning to look at her. He kept his eye on the semi fifty feet ahead. "I'm fixing it up, but I'll probably sell it."

"I remember you said you had no one to help you with Spring." She turned around to check on the baby. "Have there been any more clues about her mother?"

"No, but I'm putting an ad in the county paper today."

"Good. You need a baby-sitter to—"

"No. In the personals. To find Spring's mother."

"Oh."

He knew he should tell her about Sarah. It would be nothing to tell her the truth, but it was easier to let her go on thinking that he didn't know a condom from a wool sock. Let her go on thinking that he was involved with another woman. It kept her safely away from him. She was a woman who wanted a husband. And kids. And someone to go to chili fund-raisers with. If he said "Sarah is my little sister and I haven't seen her in five years," then things could get real complicated real fast.

The true meaning of "complicated" hit Will between the eyes an hour later, when he and Daisy stood in the baby department of North Bend's only furniture store. Spring wriggled in Daisy's arms, so

Will lifted her to his shoulder while he patted her on the back and eyed the collection of cribs.

"We have several different styles," a plump saleswoman explained. "Everything from Colonial to French Country to a lovely versatile crib that converts to a toddler bed when your baby decides she wants to sleep in a real bed."

Daisy ran a delicate hand over the top rail of a white crib with tulips painted on the sides. "They're all so pretty."

The lady looked pleased. "We have Disney characters, of course, and Winnie the Pooh, who is so popular with you young mothers nowadays. Everything is lead-free, naturally. And all of the cribs conform to today's safety standards."

Daisy checked one of the price tags and her eyebrows lifted in surprise. The saleswoman hurried to explain. "You could find one cheaper used, of course, but so many of the older cribs are unsafe." She picked up a pamphlet from a nearby changing table. "Would you like to read about it?"

"Yes," Daisy said, taking the paper. Spring started to complain, fussing loudly against Will's neck.

"Is she hungry?" The woman gestured toward a carved maple rocker. "Feel free to test out our most popular rocking chair."

Daisy shot Will a worried look. "Her bottles are out in the truck."

"I'll get one." He placed an armload of discontented baby in Daisy's arms. "Try out that rocker, will you? If she likes it, we'll get one of those, too."

The saleswoman beamed at him. "It is so nice to see the young husbands so involved these days. You hurry right back, Daddy, and we'll heat that bottle up and see if your little sweetheart likes her new furniture, all right?"

Will couldn't find words to respond. He'd never been called a "young husband" before. He glanced toward Daisy, whose cheeks looked pinker than usual, but he could only nod and get the hell out of the store. Even the word "husband" made him feel queasy, and the idea that he and Daisy looked like a young married couple just about scared him into the next county. He had to find Sarah, and he had to find her fast.

Before he started liking all this.

THE MAN DIDN'T WASTE any time doing errands, though Spring had done her fussy-baby best to complicate the entire trip to North Bend.

She couldn't help liking him. And she couldn't help remembering the way he'd kissed her. And how she'd kissed him back, like a woman starved for sex.

Which she was. But not starved enough to hop into bed with the town's most noted charming bad boy.

She would keep her mouth away from his and, as her mother always said, her "knees together." Otherwise, she could find herself the center of town gossip. And that wasn't the way to run a business or become part of a community.

"Come see the ranch," he'd said, turning off the road to town and heading north before she'd said yes or no.

So she saw the ranch house, a larger, grayer and older structure than she'd pictured. More solid, too, despite its age and obvious lack of upkeep.

"It's very big," was all she could say. When what she wanted to say was, "Paint it white, with blue shutters and fill those broken window boxes with bright pink geraniums. Plant herbs in that fenced square of ground by the south porch and hang a swing in the cottonwood between the house and the barn."

"I'm going to sell it," he explained, driving close to the back door. A brown-and-white dog ran out to greet them, his tail wagging. "That's Bozeman. You're not afraid of dogs, are you?"

"No." Just handsome cowboys who don't stay long in one place. She reached around for Spring, who looked sleepy and comfortable after the long ride. "Come here, honey. You get to try out your new bed."

He glanced down at the baby in her arms. "Do you want me to take her?"

"No. She's fine."

He took her arm anyway and helped her down from the truck. "I'll make some coffee and you can tell me what you think about where to put stuff."

"I, uh, should get back to work." Which was a lie.

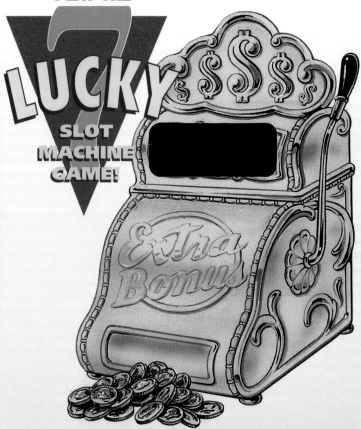

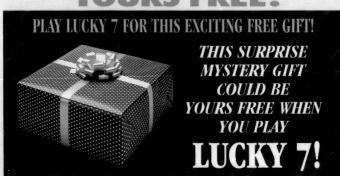

Darlene, Barlow and Heather could handle the slowest day of the week without her. They would probably be glad she wasn't bustling around, obsessing over tomorrow night's chili supper. The truth was she didn't want to spend any more time playing mommy. Heather had been right: Billy Wilson was irresistible. Almost.

She let him lead her to the back door, the friendly dog panting around her legs. She waited, protecting Spring from the cold with her blanket, while he unlocked the door and pushed it open to reveal a narrow kitchen that was surprisingly tidy, though the wall of dark-wood cabinets gave it a gloomy air until Will switched on a ceiling light.

"It's never been much," he muttered, looking around as if trying to see it with her eyes. "My mother's parents never did anything to the place except let it fall down around them."

"It's wonderful," she said, noting the planked floor and faded flowered wallpaper. The appliances were old, but they seemed to match the old-fashioned light fixtures and the wide porcelain sink. "Like something out of a movie."

"Yeah," he muttered. "*Unforgiven.*"

She peeked into the dining room, which looked more lived in than the kitchen. The square table in the middle of the room was piled high with tools and buckets. Stacks of papers and rags were mounded in corners, and coffee cups dotted the shelves of an unused hutch, as if the drinker had walked away and forgotten them. "This is where you eat?"

"No. I stand up at the kitchen counter," he said, giving her a quick smile. "This is where I've been working. Sit down and give me a minute to get the furniture inside, then I'll give you a tour." He hesitated. "Unless you need to get back right away."

It was her chance to say "Thanks, I need to work," and have him drive her to town. But it was too tempting to peek at the old Victorian home. She told herself she only wanted to make certain that Spring would have a decent place to sleep. "No," she said, stepping into what should have been a dining room. "I can stay a little while, until you get the crib set up."

"Good. Then I'll deliver you and your pizza oven to town, just in time for the supper rush."

"There's no hurry," she heard herself say, though of course there were supplies to put away and pizza ingredient portions to weigh. Portion control, she'd read, was all-important in the pizza business, and she doubted there would be free time tomorrow to test out her pizza ideas. What on earth was the matter with her? She looked down at the baby she held in her arms. Maternal hormones, that was the problem. As long as she held this baby she couldn't think clearly.

And when Will held her she couldn't think clearly, either. So naturally, if she was as smart as she liked to think she was, she would stay away from both of them and concentrate on pizza and profits. "Bring Spring's car seat in and I'll make coffee," she offered, not caring if she sounded too forward.

"Good idea." He was gone, leaving nothing but a gust of cold air as the door shut behind him and the dog that was happy to follow him back to the truck. He returned with the car seat and three big bags of baby supplies, which he deposited on the kitchen floor before returning to get the furniture.

Daisy fixed Spring in her seat and put it on the wide counter where she could see her while she rinsed out the coffeepot and searched for coffee. There wasn't much of anything in the place, so clearly Will didn't intend to stay long. Instant oatmeal packets, dog food, coffee, crackers and cans of soup barely filled one cupboard. Unmatched dishes filled another, along with scratched glasses of odd shapes and sizes. The next few minutes were filled with making the coffee and holding open the back door each time Will brought in a boxed piece of furniture.

"That's it," he declared, sliding the box that held the crib along the kitchen floor. He leaned it against the wall and shut the door behind him. He grinned. "Now comes the hard part, putting the damn thing together."

"I'll rock her until you're done." She still couldn't believe how many things he'd purchased. For a man who intended to sell this place, he'd gone to a lot of trouble to make it a home for a little while.

"Oh, no, you don't." He tossed his hat and jacket

into the dining room. "You're going to read the directions and hand me the right screwdrivers."

"I am?"

"Yes, sweetheart." He strode past her to the counter and picked up the car seat, with Spring dozing inside. "Come on," he told Daisy as he turned and headed toward the dining room. "Let me show you ladies what I've been working on."

The dining room opened onto a hallway through one door and the living room through another. Will led her into the living room. Daisy stopped short and stared.

"Do you think it still smells like paint?" Will took a deep breath as he surveyed his work. "I had the windows open for a while."

"It's fine," Daisy said, knowing her words were completely inadequate to describe what must have been an amazing transformation, if this room had been anything like the others she'd seen. The windows gleamed, the walls were freshly painted in soft ivory and the bare wood floor shone with fresh wax.

"I talked Hal into selling me some paint and caulk yesterday," Will said, setting the baby in her seat on the floor before straightening to survey his work in the late-afternoon sunlight.

"You did this in one day?"

"One night," he said. "And four pots of coffee."

"I'm impressed."

His face lit up. "Really? I wasn't sure about the

color, so I picked something Hal called 'Basic Cream' that he didn't have to mix up for me."

"Basic Cream is perfect," she said, fighting a pang of envy toward Spring's mother. Would the woman return and move in here? Would she appreciate what Will had done to make her daughter comfortable and safe?

"I'm going to move my bed down here," he said, pointing to a corner of the large, square room. "That way I'll hear her cry in the middle of the night."

Which meant Spring wouldn't be spending any more nights in Daisy's apartment, beside Daisy's bed or curled up in her arms while they rocked and watched television. She reminded herself that was a good thing. She reminded herself that she owned a restaurant and she didn't want to fall in love again. She reminded herself she liked living alone.

Most of the time.

Daisy plastered a bright smile on her face. "I'll get the coffee and we'll get started."

"Sure," he agreed, but he didn't move toward the door. Instead he stood there looking at her with an unreadable expression in his eyes. "You worried I won't be able to take care of her?"

"No, of course not. You'll do fine."

He didn't look convinced, but he started to head out of the room. "I'll get the crib."

"And I'll get the coffee," she offered, making sure that Spring was content in her seat. "I think we're going to need it."

Two hours later they dropped the new mattress

into the assembled crib. Daisy had picked out a simple washed-pine model, but at Will's urging had splurged on a pink-rosebud sheet and bumper pads, which she fixed in the crib. The new pine rocker sat in one corner of the room, and a changing table stuffed full of baby clothes sat against a nearby wall.

"Now what?"

"See if Spring likes it?"

Daisy checked on the baby. "She's asleep," she whispered. "Maybe we'd better wait. What about your bed?"

"What?"

"Don't you want to bring it down?"

"I can do it later, after I take you home."

"We could get the room finished while she's asleep," Daisy insisted. "Come on, I'll help."

"No." He tenderly moved Spring in her seat over to the corner by the rocking chair. "You stay here with her while I bring the mattress down."

Which meant she wasn't going to get to peek at the second floor. "Meaning the upstairs is off-limits?"

He flashed her a wry smile. "I hate to admit it, honey, but there's nothing about my bedroom that would interest you."

Daisy hid a sigh. Now she knew that Will Wilson was a liar.

SHE DIDN'T LIKE the bed. Daisy watched as Spring tried to lift her head and scream her displeasure at her new surroundings. Will's double-sized mattress lay against the opposite wall and, because Daisy had insisted, was covered neatly with clean sheets and a faded patchwork quilt. An armload of pillows, worn flat from years of use, was piled against the wall beside the makeshift bed.

Daisy peered over the side of the crib and patted the baby's back. "I guess pink rosebuds don't agree with her."

"She has a temper, all right," Will agreed. "It runs in the family."

"I haven't noticed your temper," she said. "What do you do? Throw things? Yell? Swear?"

"I slam doors. And I'm not Spring's father," Will said, looking down at her with those dark eyes of his. "But I guess it would be easier if everyone figured I was, so think what you want, Daisy. You've got me labeled as a man who gets laid and then leaves town—and I've got to tell you, that's really starting to get under my skin."

"You've gone to a lot of trouble for a child whose not yours. Why?"

"Joe told me that this place wasn't fit for a kid, so I figured I'd better get busy and make it right."

"And what happens if—when—Spring's mom comes back? Will you make that right, too?" The baby relaxed and put her head down, but her eyes were open as if she was trying to figure out where she was. Daisy kept patting her back.

"I figure her mother left her here, on the Triple T,

for a reason. And here she's going to stay until I can find out what's going on."

"She belongs with her family," Daisy said, lifting her chin a little, while at the same time ignoring the inner voice that said "Mind your own business." "Why are you letting everyone think she's yours?"

"You mean like when you told people my wife ran off?" His smile was brief. "I have my own reasons."

And she'd never find out what they were unless he told her. If Spring wasn't his child, then she belonged to someone he cared about. Someone he loved. Someone with a Wilson temper. "You said you didn't have any family left."

Will's lips thinned. "I said there was no one to help with Spring."

She stopped patting the baby and crossed her arms in front of her chest. "So you do have family. Someone who would have left a baby on your porch? Someone you want to protect?"

"That's enough," he said. "I might start slamming doors any minute now."

"You don't look angry."

"That's because I'm thinking about kissing you again." He took her hands and unfolded her arms from across her chest. "You might help a little," he muttered, lifting her hands to his shoulders.

"I should be getting back to work," she said, unmoving. His skin was warm through the soft flannel shirt. She moved her fingertips the tiniest bit across the material. "And I've helped you enough for one day."

"I need a lot more," he said, dipping his head to brush her lips with his own. "I'm a truly pathetic man."

"Hah," was all she could manage before his mouth touched hers again. And then there was no breath, no words, no thoughts. Just the wonderful sensation of his mouth on hers. And heat, the kind of passion that exploded without warning when she stepped closer and her body touched his. His hands were on her waist, as if to make certain she wouldn't move. He tilted his head to gain deeper access to her mouth and, with deliberate and tantalizing motions, kissed her until she forgot who he was. What he was. All Daisy knew was that her blood ran heavy and hot, settling between her legs where she leaned against Will's denim-covered thigh.

It would be so easy, she thought, letting Will move her backward, toward the mattress on the floor. So easy to satisfy this bursting need with a few tugs of his zipper and hers. Her body was already ready for him, and the bulge that grazed her abdomen proved he was as ready as she was. He'd managed to slide those wonderfully warm hands underneath her shirt and along the bare skin of her back as he'd kissed her, had searched and found the clasp of her bra.

The baby's cry brought Daisy to her senses just as she tumbled to the mattress. "No," she panted, scrambling off the bed. "I can't do this."

"She'll go to sleep," Will said, but he didn't sound convincing. They both knew that Spring slept when she wanted, which wasn't as often as anyone else would have wished.

"I can't do this, anyway," Daisy said, adjusting her clothes. "Sex always gets me in trouble."

Will climbed to his feet and grimaced as he adjusted his jeans. "You want to explain that, just in case we ever get this close again?"

"I marry the wrong men."

"Because of sex?"

"Because of great sex."

He grinned down at her. "You think it would be great, too, huh?"

Daisy brushed past him and looked around for her jacket. That nice heavy coat would protect her from all those lovely sensual reactions to his touch. "It doesn't matter, because I'm not going to let it happen. Especially not with a man who has a baby and a bad reputation. I'm not an idiot."

"No one thinks you're an idiot," Will said, hurrying after her as she headed to the kitchen. "I think you're one hell of a sexy woman."

"That's the trouble," Daisy said, lifting her suede jacket off the back of a broken chair. "I like sex and I like men and I like babies and I'd like to get married to someone who isn't humping every female who walks past his pickup truck." She picked up her purse. "Would you take me and my pizza oven home now? Please?"

"Sarah is my sister," he said, putting those strong hands on her shoulders again.

"Yeah, right," Daisy said, brushing past him. "I'll get Spring ready for the trip to town."

"It's true," he insisted. "Stay here and I'll tell you all about it."

"Before we have sex or after?"

"During, if you want."

Daisy shook her head. "Nice try, cowboy, but I'm going home now." He would never know how much willpower it took to keep her clothes on.

"I CALLED THE CAFÉ this morning and guess what? Barlow told me that Daisy went to town with Will to buy a crib."

"And you're happy about that because...?" Joe struggled to get pajamas on his particularly wiggly son while Jane leaned in the doorway of the boys' bedroom.

"Because they're doing things together, that's why."

"Only because he needs a woman's advice and you're not available."

"Liar."

Joe grinned. "Hey, it was worth a try."

"Daisy's gorgeous and single and so is Will. If ever two people were made for each other..." Her voice trailed off as the baby kicked her rib cage.

"What? Are you in labor?"

"No such luck, pal." She patted her bulging belly. "Your daughter is going to be a gymnast."

"No way. Barrel racer." He set Josh free to scramble across the floor and into the bathroom. "Why are we putting them to bed so early? It's barely six."

"I'm tired," she admitted. "They can read for a while."

"How about a back rub?"

"Think it would induce labor?"

"Maybe after a long walk?"

"I went up and down the stairs twenty times today, hoping something would happen."

He stood up and went over to wrap his arms around her. "What can I do?"

"Humor me," she said, closing her eyes and leaning against him. "I like matchmaking and I think Daisy could be a good friend. Like Will is to you. Why did he leave town and never come back?"

"That's a long story." She felt him sigh against her cheek.

"What else do I have to do?"

Joe led her over to the couch and helped her sit down, then he sat next to her and tucked her against him. "His mother moved in with her parents after her husband died. Will was about twelve, his sister—half sister, I think—was a few years younger. It wasn't a happy situation."

"I didn't know he had a sister," she said. "Does she live around here?"

"Not that I know of. Will's been trying to find her for years. One time he even hired a private investigator."

"Good heavens. Do you think she's dead?"

"Will doesn't think so."

Aha. "And would her name be Sarah?"

He sighed. "Why did I marry such a smart woman?"

"Poor guy. It hasn't made your life any easier," Jane agreed, snuggling against him. "I'm so glad there isn't a formerly pregnant former girlfriend in Will's life. That makes things so much better."

"Better for who?"

"For Daisy, of course. She can like him now."

"She likes him already."

"Mmm." Jane decided against explaining the facts of life to the poor man. Tomorrow when the boys were in play school, she and Daisy would have a talk about Will Rogers Wilson and his dysfunctional family.

And maybe, if she was very lucky, she'd go into labor immediately afterward.

"I'm going to put the boys to bed," Joe said, kissing the top of her head before he slid off the couch. "Promise me you'll stay out of this. Will and Daisy can manage just fine on their own. Besides, that cowboy has enough to deal with right now."

"Exactly," Jane said, agreeing to the fact that Will was overwhelmed. If Joe thought that she was agreeing to mind her own business, then her husband just didn't know her very well. "Your father has a lot to learn," she told her belly. "But he means well."

8

HIS SISTER. Sarah was his sister? During the time Daisy and Barlow cleared a spot on the counter for the pizza oven and put away the food supplies, Daisy had little time to think about Will's words.

And Will's kisses.

There'd been nothing said between her and Will on the way back to town, mostly because Spring kept fussing and Daisy tried to keep her mind on baby-sitting instead of wondering what Will would feel like inside her. From the smoldering looks the man had given her, she had the feeling he was wondering the same thing.

By the time she closed up the quiet restaurant and crawled into her cold and lonely bed at nine o'clock that evening, Daisy refused to think that Will might have a sister who had a baby who was left on Will's doorstep last Sunday morning.

It made him entirely too appealing. And too available. "Sexy, appealing, charming and available" was a combination that Daisy knew she should avoid, if she wanted to keep her clothes on and her pride intact.

The best thing would be to stay away from him. The next time what's-his-name, Leroy, came into the café for lunch, Daisy would be nice to him. Hint that she was available. And turn her thoughts and her body to dating the kind of man who knew who his kids belonged to, and whose cupboards held enough ingredients to make a decent meal.

"I'VE GOT TO hand it to you," Joe said, setting his end of Will's oak bed frame onto the living-room floor. "This place is starting to look pretty damn good."

"It's not bad," Will said, thinking of Daisy. He would have liked to have finished what they'd started on the mattress yesterday. He'd like to drive to town and haul her back to his bed.

"Well, once we get the bed set up..." Joe's words trailed off. "Are you listening to me?"

"Yeah. The bed." Was it possible to become addicted to the scent of a woman's skin?

"Once we get this bed set up," Joe repeated, "it will look like you're starting to make this place your home."

"Yeah, right," Will snorted, bending down to attach the rails. "Now that really would be a miracle."

"It's never too late," his friend said, surveying the room. He smiled at the baby. "No word from Sarah?"

"Nothing. I keep thinking she'll call, but she hasn't. Not even a wrong number on the answering machine. I don't understand how someone can just vanish like that."

Joe looked like he felt just as bad about Sarah as

Will did. "I've put feelers out around some other counties and I've checked the hospitals, but I haven't come up with a thing."

"She wants to stay gone, I guess."

"Or she's afraid to come home."

"Afraid of me? Why?"

Joe shrugged. "Maybe she thinks you'll be mad at her."

"I put an ad in the personals," he said, picking up one end of the mattress. "I told her it was okay."

"Yeah," Joe said, lifting his end of the mattress and helping Will position it onto the frame. "It's all going to work out just fine. Most things do. In time."

Will didn't agree, but he kept his mouth shut. Joe was only trying to make him feel better. "I should talk to a real-estate agent. Is your uncle still in the business?"

"Don't do anything right away," Joe urged. "If you sell out, Sarah won't know where to find you."

"Meaning I'm stuck on the Triple T again."

"It's not such a bad place. Lots of folks would give their eyeteeth for a spread like this one, with or without the house."

"They're welcome to it." Will looked across the room at the sleeping child. "As soon as Sarah comes back for Spring."

"THERE'S ENOUGH CHILI here to feed all of Montana and half of the Dakotas, too," Barlow insisted, waving his wooden spoon toward the walk-in cooler.

"Plus, people are bringing their own for the contest. You're worrying about nothing."

Daisy was worried about everything. She wasn't sure she had enough bowls, spoons, soda pop, napkins or extra-hot sauce to feed the people who would show up tonight. She wanted—she needed—everything to be perfect. The basketball team needed money to go to the play-offs and Daisy wanted so much to feel part of the community. "Maybe I should chop more onions."

"I already did extra." He moved the chopping knife out of her reach and slid the cutting board into a sink filled with soapy water.

"Shredded cheddar?"

"Done."

"What if I don't have enough bowls?"

He pointed to the stacks of plastic bowls behind the counter. "You have enough for the entire county and then some."

"Ice?"

"The grocery store is donating extra, remember?" He paused. "There's one thing you might need, though."

Daisy waited. "What?"

"Valium. Before you drive me crazy."

"I just want everything to go well." Maybe volunteering to host this fund-raiser hadn't been such a brilliant idea. Next time she'd keep her mouth shut when she went to the chamber of commerce meeting. Maybe next time she'd pick a less stressful business than running a restaurant. Like a jet-fighter pilot. Or a brain surgeon.

Heather poked her head in the door. "Daisy, someone wants to see you."

"Not him." And not now, when her resolutions to resist all that dangerous charm were fresh in her mind. She'd even managed to get a good night's sleep, despite missing Spring. Funny how the rooms felt so empty.

The waitress gave her a blank look. "Him who?"

"Never mind. I'll be right there." She turned back to Barlow. "You're sure we're all set?"

He checked his watch. "Six hours until the big event? I think we can handle it. Go drink some tea or something. Just get out of my kitchen for a while."

Daisy slipped her order pad in the pocket of her apron. "I guess I'd better go be a waitress for a while."

"Good. I'm going to eat breakfast before the lunch rush starts." Barlow waved goodbye and turned back to the grill to flip flapjacks. "You want anything?" he called over his shoulder.

"No, thanks." She was too nervous to eat. Which was ridiculous. She'd been through worse before, when she'd worked in Wyoming. Like the time the power went off in the middle of feeding twenty-eight passengers off the Greyhound bus. Or when the mean-looking drifter tried to rob the cash register at closing time. Daisy took a deep breath and left the kitchen.

"Daisy?" Jane waved from a corner booth. She

still looked very pregnant and very healthy and very happy. Daisy swallowed her envy and hurried over to the booth.

"Hi. How are you feeling?"

"Like a truck full of hogs," she moaned. "Can you sit for a minute?"

She glanced around the nearly empty room. Heather obviously had everything under control. The young woman even had time to flirt with her latest boyfriend, who was seated on a stool at the counter. "Sure. Do you want some coffee or anything?"

"Maybe later." Jane grinned at her. "I have something really interesting to tell you—Sarah is Will's sister."

"I know."

Jane's face fell. "Damn. Here I thought I had some really hot information."

Daisy laughed. "He told me, but I didn't believe him. Not until now."

"He told you? That's interesting."

"Why?"

Jane tried to lean forward, but gave up. "Haven't you been married twice?"

"Yes."

"And you still don't know anything about men?" Jane laughed. "Come on, Daisy. He wouldn't have told you if he didn't want you to know he wasn't, um, involved with some other woman. He must care what you think about him."

Daisy wasn't convinced. She didn't think Will

Wilson cared too much what people thought. "Will's not like that."

"You picked out the crib yesterday?"

"A white one, very simple and sweet. And a beautiful rosebud-print blanket and bumper pads." Daisy leaned on her elbow. "He's fixed up his living room for a bedroom."

"I heard. Joe went out this morning to help him move stuff around."

"He had to move the bed," Daisy said, remembering the way she'd tumbled onto the mattress within minutes of being kissed.

"You're blushing," Jane pointed out. "Don't worry. I'm not going to ask—"

"Daisy McGregor," Maude Anderson hollered, crossing the room at a surprising pace for an elderly lady. "You're just the person I want to see!"

"I am?" She looked at Jane, who shrugged.

"I've been thinking about this," Maude said, sitting down next to Jane, who had obligingly managed to slide over to make room. "Ever since Hazel told me about Billy Wilson being left alone with that sweet baby. How are they doing?"

"Just fine. Really." She ignored Jane's curious look. "Couldn't be better."

"He bought her a new crib," Jane added as if she couldn't wait to see what happened next.

Maude looked disappointed. "With blankets?"

"Yes," Daisy said, "but why—"

"Darn it all to heck, I told Hazel we'd better get on the stick and get this put together real soon. But no, she had to ask Martha's opinion and it takes two days to get that woman to make up her mind about pink or yellow borders." Maude leaned forward and looked at Daisy. "Pink, I said. Don't you agree?"

"For what?"

"The quilt. We got together and whipped up a little quilt top last night. Nothing fancy, mind you, but plenty nice, since June Briggs had some pretty little nine-patch squares all done up already, just for an emergency."

Jane smiled. "You made Spring a quilt? That's so nice."

Maude patted her hand. "I just know that pink one we gave you and Joe is going to come in handy this time. Do you have a name picked out if it's a girl?"

"Hannah, I think," Jane mused. "Do you think that's too old-fashioned?"

"It's lovely, just lovely," Maude said, and turned back to Daisy. "So, what do you think?"

"I like the name," she said. "I have an aunt—"

"Not about Hannah," Maude said, wagging a finger at her. "The quilt. When should we give it to him?"

"I think that's up to you," Daisy replied. "But I'm sure Will would be very happy to—"

"No," Maude said. "We can't have the shower at his house. I can just imagine how that miserable grandfather of his left that place. No, we thought we'd have it here, since the two of you are such good friends and you've been helping with the baby." She turned to Jane. "I have to say, I hope that no-good wife of his stays away from town. Can you imagine leaving a baby like that, in the care of a rodeo man? What could she have been thinking?"

Jane's eyebrows rose. "I don't think—"

"—we should be talking about her," Daisy finished, giving Jane a warning look.

Her new friend only look amused as she answered the older lady. "You want to have a baby shower for Spring, Mrs. Anderson?"

"Yes. That poor little motherless babe most likely needs a few things to welcome her to the community. And we thought we'd have it here."

"Here? In the café?"

"That way Billy won't feel too overwhelmed by so many women."

"I don't think that's a problem for him," Daisy murmured.

"What a good idea," Jane agreed. "The café is the perfect place."

"Is Friday afternoon good? There'll be about ten of us, maybe more if June gets the word out. Maybe you could have a soup-and-sandwich special that day—nothing too heavy, though—and I'll get a sheet cake from the supermarket."

"Oh, let me do that," Jane said. "I'll order it today and if I happen to be having a baby by Friday, someone else can pick it up."

"That would be lovely," Maude agreed. She

smiled at Daisy. "Now you'll make sure he's here on Friday, at noon?"

"Me?"

"You," Jane said, barely hiding her amusement. "Since you're one of his closest friends."

Maude nodded and reached over to pat Daisy's hand. "Just be careful, dear. Billy has always been a wild boy. Attracted the girls like flies to honey. Still, if his wife has really left him." She looked at Daisy through narrowed eyes. "He may be ready to settle down."

"Which is none of my business," Daisy insisted. "Really, it's not. We're barely even friends and I was only helping out with Spring because he didn't know anything about babies."

Maude released Daisy's hand and shook her head. "Dear, what man does?" She scooted out of the booth, almost bumping into Heather, who'd come over to the table, her order pad in her hand. "I'll leave some corn bread for Heather for tonight. I'm not coming back later. Chili doesn't agree with me."

"Thank you," Daisy called.

"She can't hear you," Jane said. "Not unless you're in close range."

Heather stepped up to the table. "You want some tea or coffee or anything?"

Daisy turned to Jane. "Can you stay for a few minutes?"

"Sure, if you're going to sit and drink a cup of tea with me." She looked at her watch as the waitress hurried off to the counter to fix their drinks. "I don't have to pick up the boys for another hour and I still have to buy some groceries. What about you? Do you have time to tell me about Will's wife?"

"I made it up, because the women were all gossiping about it over lunch, so I told them his wife suffered from postpartum depression and disappeared."

Jane began to laugh. "Well, it worked. Does he know?"

"Yes. He wasn't too pleased, but I think he's been too busy with the baby to care."

"It's all going to work out," Jane insisted, still looking as if she wanted to burst into laughter. She looked very cheerful for someone who was overdue to have a baby.

"What do you mean?"

"Spring's going to get a quilt, which is a time-honored town tradition. It's bound to be gorgeous, too, because those ladies sure know how to quilt."

"It's very sweet. I feel so guilty."

"Don't. Spring deserves it. But when you start dating Will, the whole town will think you're going out with a married man."

"She's not going out with Billy Wilson," Heather said, setting two mugs of tea on the table. "She's determined to date Leroy."

Jane stared at Daisy as if she'd lost her mind. "Leroy Doyle? Why?"

Heather answered for her. "She likes kids, and he's got three of them. If you ask me, I think old

Leroy is just looking for help with those teenagers of his. And maybe some home cooking, too. He probably thinks because you run a café that you know how to cook."

"I do know how to cook," Daisy insisted, "but that's not the point. Thanks for the tea," she said, hoping the young woman would get the hint and go back to the counter to talk to the young man who was pretending not to watch her.

"Anytime, boss." Heather looked at Jane. "Talk some sense into her, Mrs. Pierce. Who'd pick Leroy Doyle over Billy Wilson?"

Jane opened a sugar packet into her cup. "That's exactly what I want to know."

"A sensible woman," Daisy said, taking a careful sip of tea. "A woman who has tangled with too many cowboys and who would be a fool to do it again."

"I see," Jane said, once again looking as if she was trying not to laugh. "This is the same sensible woman who took a stranger's baby—and the stranger—home with her last Sunday night?"

"From now on, I'm going to say no," she promised. "I'm getting too old for this kind of nonsense."

For some reason that only made Jane laugh harder.

THE WILLIE NELSON SONG, the one about not letting your babies grow up to be cowboys, rang in Will's ears. It had been the last song on the radio as he had driven into Safeway's parking lot and pulled the truck into a spot by the supermarket's front door.

"That's good advice," he told Spring, who gave him a look that said: *Get me out of this car seat before I start screaming.* It was a look Will and his eardrums had come to respect. "Uncle Will doesn't want you getting into trouble with any young men, whether they're cowboys or not," he told her, hoping that conversation would delay the inevitable hollering of a baby who wanted either dry pants or a warm bottle. If he could get some groceries before Spring got too upset, then he could head over to the café and see if he could persuade Daisy to help him out.

Which she might not do, considering yesterday's disaster. Okay, so it hadn't been the smartest thing to tumble Daisy McGregor onto his mattress and attempt to remove her bra in the process. He should have shown more restraint. But she'd kissed him back, and those soft, ample breasts had pillowed right against him and the next thing he knew he was lying on the mattress, figuring that Daisy's lush body was going to be his.

"Ahhhhh," Spring squeaked, frowning up at him as he untangled the car seat straps from around her.

"Don't kiss any cowboys, either, not unless you mean business," he told the infant. "We're a hot-blooded lot, you see, and it doesn't take much to get—oh, hi there, Mrs. Briggs." He tucked Spring against his chest and, congratulating himself on how good he was getting at dealing with this one-handed stuff, managed to lock the truck and show off his baby to one of the gray-haired old biddies of the town.

"She's got the look of your mother around the eyes," Mrs. Briggs declared, then eyed Will. "I hear her mother ran off and left you."

"Yes, ma'am," Will said through gritted teeth.

"You're better off without a woman like that," she said, and surprised him by patting his arm. "You'll do fine, Billy. Your mother always said that you'd come home and settle down some day."

"She did? I didn't know you—"

"Talked about you?" June Briggs nodded. "She joined our canasta group some years back, after your grandmother died. I think she liked getting off the ranch and playing cards once a week."

He'd forgotten about that. "She liked going to town."

"What about that sister of yours? Do you ever hear from her?"

"Once in a while," Will fibbed, and then changed his mind. "I'm trying to find her right now."

Mrs. Briggs touched the baby's cheek with one gnarled finger. "You could use the help, I suppose," she said. "The McGregor woman has a business to run and doesn't seem much like the ranch-wife type."

"No," Will said, unsure if he was agreeing or not. He watched as Mrs. Briggs managed to back out her old Chrysler without hitting any other cars and then, Spring tucked firmly against his chest, he hurried into the store, the words "ranch wife" echoing ominously in his head.

He wanted to sleep with Daisy, not put a wedding ring on her finger. Which made him wince. But hell, one week of baby-sitting couldn't turn him into Joe Pierce.

DAISY HEARD SPRING before she saw her. She'd just placed another bowl of chopped onions on the serving table underneath the window when she saw Will step inside the café, the screaming baby in his arms. Not that anyone noticed, with the crowd that was stuffed inside the room. The basketball team could be pleased that the fund-raiser was such a success.

Will frowned as he approached her. "What the hell is going on here? Half the town—" He paused when a blond-haired cheerleader asked him for a five-dollar donation to the chili supper. "Sure, honey," he said, handing Daisy the baby so he could get his wallet out of his jeans pocket.

"Thanks, Mr. Wilson," she said. "If you want to buy a raffle ticket you can go see my mother, over there in the corner."

Will looked stunned. "Darlene's old enough to have a teenage daughter?"

Daisy handed the baby back to him. "None of us is getting any younger. And this stinky baby needs a clean diaper."

"That's why I came," he said, turning to show her

the diaper bag hitched over his shoulder. "See? I'm prepared."

"Prepared to do it yourself, I hope," Daisy said, trying to edge away. Just standing too close to him did strange things to intimate parts of her body. She'd been alone too long, she told herself. And she was way too susceptible to handsome men. "You can use the apartment if you want."

"Hey, thanks." He smiled, that sexy smile she'd noticed the first time she'd seen him. "Can you come, too?"

"I'm busy."

"Doing what?"

"Refilling condiments." She pulled her key chain from her apron pocket and handed it to him. "There you go."

"Aren't you afraid someone will talk?" He dangled it from his index finger for all the world to see.

"Too late." Daisy decided she'd tell him about the baby shower later, when Spring wasn't hollering at the top of her lungs. "You'd better go before she turns any redder."

He glanced down at her. "A few days ago this would have bothered me. Now I'm standing here flirting with you while she has a fit."

"We're not flirting."

Will smiled again. "If I tell you that you're gorgeous when your hair is falling down your neck and you have tiny beads of sweat on your forehead and your lips look like you need to be kissed, is that flirting?"

"Yes," Daisy said, hoping she wasn't blushing because several people had started to stare at them. "And if I told you that yesterday was a mistake and from now on you'd better keep your distance, what would you call that?"

Will Wilson didn't blink. He went on giving her that lazy once-over while the baby cried and he bent down and whispered. "Why, honey, I'd call that a challenge."

"Good luck with that diaper," she called as he turned around and headed for the front door. She hoped it was the smelliest and nastiest diaper that had ever existed. Daisy surveyed the chili table to make sure everything was in order before she returned to the kitchen. Leroy hadn't shown up yet, but when he and his kids arrived, she'd make sure to give him another chance.

"LOOKS LIKE you've got a rival," Joe said.

Will gave Spring to a mature-looking teenage girl, along with ten dollars. "Are you sure you know how to hold her?"

"I have three younger sisters, Mr. Wilson," she said, taking the baby to a booth where several other teenagers waited.

"They've started to call me Mr. Wilson," he said. "God, that sounds old."

"Pay attention, Will." Joe nodded toward the counter, where seven men sat on stools. One of the men was deep in conversation with a smiling Daisy, who looked only too pleased to refill his coffee for him. "Doyle is a man who needs a wife."

"Why?" Will glanced in that direction, but only saw a heavyset man with graying hair above the collar of a brown flannel shirt. Daisy stood across the counter from him and seemed to be paying attention to his conversation.

"He's a widower with three teenagers. He's been trying to get Daisy to go out with him since the first day she took over the café."

"She never said yes?"

"Nope, not that I know of, but I wouldn't bet money against it tonight."

Will swore under his breath. "If he touches her I'll kick his—"

"Don't make threats in front of the sheriff," Joe said, trying to keep a straight face. He looked over at Jane and winked.

"She's mine," Will declared, realizing as he said it that he'd never meant anything more. He watched Daisy carefully to make sure she wasn't standing too close to that jerk.

"Does the lady know that?"

"Not yet, but she will. Later. In private."

Joe let out the breath he'd been holding. "Good. I didn't want to have to break up a fight on my night off." He managed to sneak a thumbs-up sign to his wife without Will noticing. "So what are you going to do?"

"Take her home."

"She's not a puppy."

Will didn't appreciate the joke. "Why is she smiling at him?"

Joe shrugged. "Jane says Daisy wants to settle down with a family man. And you're not exactly the type." He hesitated before adding, "Or are you?"

"I've got a ranch, a dog, three horses and a baby. I'd say I'd qualify."

"You don't have the wedding ring," Joe said. "You don't *want* the wedding ring."

"That's the last thing I want or need," Will muttered. "But I want that woman. And Doyle can't have her."

"If I didn't know better, I'd think you sounded like a man in love."

"Who's talking about love?" Will didn't take his gaze from Daisy, even when she looked up and saw him watching her. That defiant chin lifted and she deliberately turned away, but Will knew she was still thinking about last night. Or he hoped she was.

Joe laughed. "You've got it bad."

"I'm fine," Will insisted. "And it has nothing to do with love and wedding rings." But it had everything to do with the way Daisy kissed him and the way she felt in his arms.

Nothing more.

9

"DAISY, HONEY," Will purred, stepping up close to touch his lips to her forehead in an intimate manner. "Thanks again for the help with the bed yesterday."

He made "bed" sound like "sex," for heaven's sake. Daisy stepped away from him, but bumped into the edge of the counter. "It was nothing," she said, hoping that the men seated on nearby stools weren't listening. She glanced toward them on the pretense of checking their glasses. "Anyone need more water?"

Leroy lifted his glass. "I do, thanks."

The man next to him shook his head. "How you can eat that sh—stuff from Ellie Carson I'll never know. It's got no flavor. Aren't you going to put some more hot sauce in it?"

"Some men don't like it hot, Charlie," Will said over Daisy's head, so she gave him an elbow in the ribs.

"Excuse me, Will." Daisy refilled Leroy's glass and gave the quiet man a quick smile. He was nice enough, if you liked the kind of man who never said much of anything. Leroy had kind eyes, but he looked like a man who'd accepted being beaten down by the world.

"Thanks." Leroy took a couple of long swallows of the water, then put down the glass and looked at Daisy. He opened his mouth as if he was going to speak, but then he picked up his spoon again and looked down into the bowl.

"You're welcome," Daisy said, giving up for now. She went along the counter and refilled everyone's water, whether they needed it or not. Anything to get away from Will and his deliberate attempts to embarrass her. "Have you all bought raffle tickets?"

"I haven't," Will called. "What's the prize?"

Charlie swiveled to look over at him. "Hey there, Billy. You could win one of the ladies' quilts or an oil change and two new tires at the garage. Take your pick."

"Sounds good," he said, pulling his wallet out. "Where do I buy a ticket?"

Daisy pointed to the other side of the room. "Over there. Where's the baby?"

"I hired a baby-sitter." He looked at Leroy. "How many kids do you have now, Doyle?"

Leroy looked surprised that Will would talk to him. "Three," he said, turning back to his chili.

"Interesting guy," Will said in a low voice only Daisy could hear.

"Go away," she whispered. "I'm working."

Will raised his voice enough to be heard in the next county. "I'll be back," he said. "But I sure hope I win that quilt. You know how short of blankets I am."

He winked, then to Daisy's relief turned around and waded into the crowd. The chili supper was definitely a success, she realized. And everyone looked as if they were having a good time. Most folks had stayed long after they'd eaten supper because the high-school cheerleaders were selling brownies and cookies for dessert and the Booster Club wouldn't pick the prizewinning tickets until seven-thirty. And then the votes would be counted and the winning chili chef would be announced. Barlow was sure he was going to win. Every time Daisy looked his way, he made a V-for-victory sign.

"I told you so," Heather said, coming up beside her to make a fresh pot of coffee.

"Told me what?" She watched as Will bent over the raffle table and flirted with the two middle-aged women with the cash box and tickets.

"About Billy Wilson. He's the sexiest man over thirty in this whole boring town."

"He thinks he is."

"You're looking at him like he is," Heather informed her. "By the time the chili's gone, everyone in town is going to assume you're sleeping with him."

Daisy hurried to turn her back on the crowd. "Are you kidding?"

"Nope."

"I'm not—" She remembered to lower her voice, not that anyone could hear them with the amount of noise in the place. "I'm not sleeping with him."

"You will be," the young woman assured her. "And you have to promise to tell me all about it."

"I will not," Daisy said as Heather picked up a coffee carafe and went into the crowd to pour refills. "Because nothing is going to happen."

Heather sighed. "You probably wouldn't tell me anyway, huh?"

"That's right." But it wasn't going to happen, she promised herself. So why did she feel so disappointed?

"BEHAVE YOURSELF."

"What makes you think I'm not?" Will tucked his wallet back into his jeans and grinned at his best friend's wife. He liked Jane a lot, envied the kind of marriage his friends had made.

"You're up to no good," she said, taking his arm. "You look like one of my boys when he's trying to get away with something."

"Are we going somewhere?"

"You're helping me over to that chair over there, then you're going to lower me into it. I'd ask Joe, but he's disappeared, probably patrolling the parking lot or something."

"You okay?"

"I'm fine, just tired."

"I can take you home."

"And miss watching you glare at poor Leroy Doyle whenever Daisy talks to him? No way."

"He can't have her."

"He can if she wants him to."

Will eased Jane into the chair. "How are you going to get up?"

"I'm not." She sighed. "I wish this little girl would hurry up and be born."

"It's a girl?" Spring would have a playmate. The thought tickled him, until he remembered he would be leaving town soon. Sarah couldn't stay away forever, and he couldn't spend the rest of his life waiting for her to show up.

"I hope."

"You want coffee or a Coke or anything?"

"You can't just have sex with her and then ride off into the sunset. It doesn't always work that way."

It had so far, but Will decided not to say so. "Seems like everyone around here is real interested in my sex life. I should have remembered that about this damn town."

"People around here think you're very interesting," Jane explained. "You're a rodeo star, you inherited that old ranch and now you've got a little baby and a missing wife."

Will watched Daisy lean across the counter to admire Spring, who was being carried around by the enthusiastic teenager he'd hired. "She sure likes babies."

Jane looked across the room. "Yes, and she likes you. So behave yourself."

"We're mature adults, Janie," he said.

"One of you is." Jane gave him a gentle push. "I give up. Go annoy Daisy some more and see if that gets you anywhere. And if you see Joe, send him over, okay?"

"Yeah." He hesitated. "Are you sure you're okay? You look a little pale."

She groaned. "I'm supposed to be glowing."

"You're not?"

"Not tonight," Jane promised, patting her swollen belly.

"Not tonight," was exactly what Daisy told him ten minutes later when he asked her if he and Spring could come over after the chili supper was finished. "I may have a date."

He crooked a finger toward Doyle, who was busy buying a handful of brownies. "With him?"

"Maybe. But that's none of your business." She made a big show out of ignoring him while she refilled a napkin dispenser.

"Everything's everybody's business in this town. So far tonight seven different people have asked me about my 'wife' and my baby and when I'm going to sell the ranch and if I am, what am I going to ask for it and if I'm moving in with you—"

"What?"

He laughed at the shocked expression on her face. "No, I'm only kidding about that last part, but it's only a matter of time."

She gazed at him as if she was deep in thought. "What are you doing Friday afternoon?"

"You're asking me out?"

Daisy shrugged and gave him a little smile. "Just answer the question."

"I can be free. What time?"

"Come here at noon. Not a minute before." She reached for a cloth and began wiping down the counter. "And bring the baby."

"Okay, but—" He saw Joe heading toward him through the crowd, so he waved and pointed in Jane's direction. The sheriff nodded and changed direction.

"What's all that about?"

"Jane wants to go home," he explained. "How long is this thing going to last?"

She looked at her watch. "It's just about over. They're going to announce the winners of the raffle and then crown a Chili King." She gestured toward Barlow, who had come out of the kitchen to talk to the various customers milling around the raffle table. "I think he's campaigning for the title."

"We have a winner for the new tires and lube job!" Darlene held up a ticket, which pretty much silenced the crowd "Ned Sanderson, come up here and get your gift certificate!"

"Mr. Wilson?" Will turned to see Spring and her baby-sitter behind him. "She's not happy anymore."

"Thanks for helping out." Will took the baby in his arms at the exact moment she screamed her anger at whatever it was she was angry with. He felt at least a hundred pairs of eyes on him, but pretended everything was okay as he put the baby to his shoulder and patted her back. "It's okay, honey," he said, keeping his voice low. "These people can't bother us, no sir."

Darlene put her hand back into the raffle box for the quilt and pulled out another card. "And the lucky owner of the quilt donated by the Ladies' Aid Society is Daisy McGregor!"

Will hid his grin as Daisy stepped forward and looked very confused. "But I didn't buy a ticket," she admitted. "I was so busy that I forgot and—"

"Your name's right here, honey," the president of the Booster Club said, handing her the winning ticket and the quilt.

"Well, thank you very much," she managed to say, touching the blue and white fabric with reverent fingertips, as if she was afraid the whole thing might explode. Will would have laughed, but he was too busy trying to keep Spring from screaming again. He bounced her up and down a little, hoping the jiggling motion would distract her long enough for him to find the diaper bag and get out of town before Daisy changed her mind about Friday.

"THREE HUNDRED AND FIFTY dollars?" Daisy dropped the crepe-paper streamer she'd been trying to fasten to the corner of the window. "You're kidding!"

Jane lowered herself into a booth. "Nope. Marie Johnson told me that Darlene told her that he'd bought seventy packets of tickets. It took four people to fill them all out and he made sure they wrote your name. I guess Will really wanted you to win.

"It was the most successful raffle the town's had in years." She looked around the café at the decorations for the baby shower. "Where did you get all this stuff?"

"People have been dropping things off for two days," she explained, fastening another piece of pink crepe paper to the top corner of the front window. "Do you think it's too much?"

"Well, yes, but that's the way it's supposed to look, isn't it?"

"I suppose so," Daisy said, stepping down from the chair she'd been standing on. She looked at her watch. "They should start arriving any minute now. Where are your boys?"

"At school, then they're going home with a friend of mine to play. I couldn't miss this event."

"He's going to be furious."

Jane laughed. "Oh, I know. That's why it's going to be so much fun."

Daisy wondered how one man could be so annoying and so intriguing at the same time. "I can't keep that quilt."

"Sure you can. You won it, fair and square."

"He wouldn't even let me talk to him about it," Daisy complained. "He took that baby and flung the diaper bag over his shoulder and left without a word, except to tell me he'd see me Friday."

"How did you get him to come here?"

"I invited him."

Jane's eyes widened. "He thinks it's a date?"

"Of course not." She unwound another strand of

crepe paper from the roll. "I told him to bring the baby. He thinks I'm fixing him lunch."

HE THOUGHT Daisy had finally come to her senses. He thought he was finally going to get her clothes off her. When he walked into the front door of the café, Spring tucked firmly against his shoulder, he barely noticed anything out of the ordinary. Will was too busy thinking about Daisy to notice that the inside of the restaurant looked different.

Oh, he thought there were a lot more women in the place than usual. Older, gray-haired women especially, he realized as he strode across the room to greet Daisy at the lunch counter, which was crowded with customers. "Hey, honey," he said, giving her his best here-I-am smile.

"Well, hi," she said, looking nervous. "You two are right on time."

"You ready to go?"

"Go where?"

He frowned. "Wherever you want. You asked me, remember?"

She glanced past him and waved to someone, but Will didn't bother to turn around to see who. "Yes, so I think you'd better—"

"I kept her awake all morning so she'd sleep this afternoon," he said, turning slightly to show her the sleepy baby.

"Hi, honey," Daisy cooed, looking a lot happier to see the baby than to see the man. Then she looked up at him. "You're not going to like this," she said, but Will thought she was trying not to laugh.

"Not going to like what?"

"Before you turn around, put a smile on your face and look happy to be here," Daisy said.

Damn. This wasn't going the way he'd planned. The vision of Daisy leading him into her apartment vanished. "Why?"

"For Spring," she said, and gave him a little shove so he'd turn.

"Surprise!" a chorus of voices said. Will saw a sea of old ladies coming toward him, their gazes fixed on his baby. Jane Pierce, looking larger than ever, stood nearby and winked at him.

"What the hell?"

"Shh," Daisy warned, giving him an elbow in the side. "Be nice. They've gone to a lot of trouble."

"For what?"

"This is a baby shower," Maude Anderson explained, lifting Spring out of Will's arms. "Let's get this little darling unwrapped so we can see her."

Will watched his wide-eyed baby being taken over by a dozen grandmothers. "What's going on, Daisy?"

She waved toward the pink streamers hanging from the window. "The Ladies' Aid Society welcomes every baby in town with its own quilt. They wanted to do this for Spring."

"Why?"

"Because she's part of the town now," Daisy explained. "Until her mother comes back."

"And if she doesn't come back?" Which was something he'd never let himself think about. Until now.

"I guess that's up to you," she said, giving him a little push toward the center tables where the ladies were gathered. "Go on. I'll serve lunch as soon as they get seated."

"So this isn't a date." He noticed that some of the men were listening to their conversation, so he lowered his voice.

"No."

"Just tell me you're not going out with Doyle."

"Leroy was more interested in food than in me last night," Daisy said, looking ridiculously disappointed. "So he didn't ask."

"Good," Will said, ignoring Maude calling for him. "Then you're free tonight."

"I can't—"

"You owe me," he began, but she interrupted.

"For the quilt? No way. Take it back."

For a second he didn't understand what she was talking about. "Not the quilt. What would I need with something like that? No, I'm talking about this afternoon." He smiled down into those gorgeous blue eyes of hers. "You led me to believe that we were going to be alone."

She blushed. He loved it when she did that.

"The ladies are waiting," she reminded him.

No way was he going to leave her, not without a promise for tonight. "You set me up."

"You deserved it after the way you acted around Leroy."

He wanted to kiss her. Actually he wanted to haul her into the back room and make love to her against the wall. "Later," he said, his voice low. "We'll go out to dinner."

She shook her head. "It's pizza night."

"Billy, come on over here!" Maude hollered over the noise of chattering women.

"I'll be right there," he said, giving her a polite smile. "Get someone else to make pizza," he insisted.

"No," Daisy said, moving away from him to grab the coffee carafe.

"Just tell me one thing," he said, waiting for her to look at him.

"What?"

"Did you sleep under the quilt last night?" She nodded. "Good," he said, stepping closer so he could whisper into her ear. "I pictured you naked and warm and lonely under that quilt. Was I right?"

"You got two out of three, cowboy," she said, and started refilling coffee cups.

Which meant she was either cold or wearing pajamas, but she damn well couldn't have been with another man, Will decided as he headed toward the Ladies' Aid Society members. His mother would have loved this. Will's gaze went to Spring, whose body was cradled against June Briggs's massive bosom. His mother would have loved this baby, no matter where she came from, because she was

Sarah's. He hoped his little sister would come home soon, because if he didn't get out of this town soon he was sure to go stark raving mad.

OF COURSE Spring needed her. If Daisy didn't know better, she'd think the little charmer was in cahoots with her uncle. "Give her to me," she heard herself say as she reached for the screaming baby. "I'll change her."

"Here," Will said, handing her the diaper bag by its strap. "I remembered it again. Pretty good, huh?"

"Downright miraculous," she said, turning toward the back room and her apartment. "I'll be back in a few minutes."

"Can I come, too?"

"Go around," she said, knowing that everyone in town already knew they were friends and probably assumed they were a lot more than that. They would have been, too, if she hadn't come to her senses the other afternoon. "I'll unlock the kitchen door."

She told Heather she was taking a break, hurried through the back room and unlocked the door to her apartment. Will was already waiting at the rear door. "That was quick," she said, opening the door for him. He followed her into the living room and she set the baby on the couch and proceeded to change her. "So you survived your first baby shower?"

"Yeah. It wasn't so bad. Spring liked the attention."

"I noticed that both of you looked like you were having a good time."

He grinned. "I haven't been around that many women at one time since the last Miss Texas Rodeo pageant."

"I suppose you enjoyed yourself then, too," she said, feeling a very unaccustomed stab of envy. "Did your date win?"

"Sure," he said. "I was one of the judges."

She had to laugh. "I should have known."

"Not because of me," he said. "It was a unanimous vote from a six-judge panel. That gal could sing the 'Star Spangled Banner' better than anyone I ever heard in my life."

Daisy decided not to ask any more questions. She refastened Spring's one-piece sleeper and handed her to her uncle. "There," she said, looking at her watch. "It's almost three-thirty. Now I have to go back to work."

"You work too much. Take the night off and I'll buy you dinner in North Bend."

"I can't," she said, though she would have loved to eat somewhere other than the café for a change. "I'm testing pizza tonight."

"On who?"

"On whoever shows up. And I told Jane I'd bring her some for dinner. She wasn't feeling very well when she left a while ago."

"I'll see that she—"

The knocking on the door surprised them both. Daisy opened the door to Joe Pierce, who stepped inside out of the cold. Snowflakes dotted his Stetson. "Hey, Daisy, is Will still here?"

"Yeah," Will answered, stepping into the kitchen with the baby snug in his arms. "What's going on?"

"I've got some news," he said, wiping his boots on the mat inside the door. "We found an older-model truck in a ditch about twenty miles from here, along the interstate. It could be the one you heard leave your road."

"No one saw it before now?"

"Not until some of those big drifts melted," Joe said.

"Was she—"

"No. It was empty, no sign that anyone inside had been injured."

Daisy watched Will let out the breath he'd been holding. "What do we do next?"

"We'll track down the license plate and see who it leads us to. I think it's the break we've needed, Will."

"Seriously?"

"Yeah. As soon as anything turns up I'll let you know."

Daisy walked him to the door. "I'm making pizza for your supper tonight and Will's going to deliver it."

Joe gave her a worried look. "Did Jane overdo it this afternoon?"

"A little, but she went home to rest."

"I wish that baby would hurry up and get here," he said. "I'll call you later, Will, when I find out who owns that truck."

Daisy shut the door behind him and turned to Will. "That's good news."

"Is it?"

"Joe said it was."

"Joe didn't say that the driver could have been hurt, could have wandered off into the storm, could have been picked up by some son of a bitch who—"

"Stop it. You don't even know if that was her truck."

He went to the small window above the sink and looked out into the rapidly darkening sky. "It was my fault. I left first," he said, his voice so quiet Daisy wondered if he knew he spoke aloud. "I had to get out of there before something bad happened. My mother understood, but it broke her heart. And Sarah—"

Daisy moved closer and took his hand. "Come sit down," she said, urging him into the living room. She waited until he was seated before curling up next to him on the couch. "What happened to Sarah?"

"She stuck it out for seven more years—she was a lot younger than me—and was about to graduate from high school. She had a scholarship to Montana State. I bought her a car with my winnings from Denver that year."

"And then?"

He moved the sleeping baby into his right arm.

"My grandmother died and my grandfather got meaner than ever, my mother wouldn't move out and leave him alone, and then one day Sarah got in her car and drove off."

"To school?"

"No, though my mother and I tried to get her to change her mind, but Sarah wanted nothing more to do with Montana or school or anything else. She had a boyfriend." He looked down at Daisy and almost smiled. "And he'd joined the marines. That was the last we heard until Mom died. I've been trying to find her for years, even hired a detective."

"Do you think she's still with him?"

"No, that was years ago. He's married now, stationed somewhere in North Carolina, and says he hasn't talked to Sarah for a couple of years."

"And she didn't come back when your mother died?"

"No. I didn't have the funeral here anyway. I buried my mother near Bozeman, with my father. She would have wanted it that way."

"I'm sorry," she said, touching his arm.

"She would have gotten a kick out of the baby shower," he said. "Maude told me that my mother had friends in town before she died. I liked hearing that."

Daisy took her hand away from his arm. She didn't want to like him any more than she did already. "I think I'd better get back to work."

"Yeah." But neither of them moved, except for Will draping his free arm around Daisy's shoulders.

She closed her eyes, just for a few seconds, and pretended this was her man and her baby and she didn't have to go back to the café and pour coffee and make pizzas.

"Come home with me," he whispered, his arm tightening around her.

"I can't," Daisy said, but she regretted turning him down. She would have liked to pretend he was hers for a while longer.

10

"YOUR SISTER'S NOT answering. I'm going to call Will."

"No!" Jane stopped and took some deep breaths before she continued. "I don't want him over here."

"Why not? He's right in town. I just talked—"

Did she have to explain everything to this man? "It'll ruin everything and he'll never get married." Joe continued to stare at her as if she was speaking German. "The house is a mess and the boys ate too much candy at the sitter's and will either throw up half the night or they'll fight with each other and—"

"What's that got to do with anything?"

"Stop glaring at me," she said, managing to throw a new romance novel into her suitcase before she closed it. "I might have time to read after the baby's born."

"I don't remember you being like this the other times," he muttered, taking the suitcase off the bed. "I'm calling Will. He can stay here until I can get hold of your sister."

"It'll ruin him for marriage," she moaned, and then was hit with another contraction that almost knocked her to her knees. She clung to the bedpost and remembered to count.

"He was ruined a long time ago," Joe assured her, reaching for the bedside phone.

"Touch that phone and I'll have to hurt you."

Joe ignored her. "I love you, too, honey." He hit the speed dial. "Hey, Barb, get me the café, will you? We're heading to North Bend to have a baby."

"You don't have to tell the world," Jane muttered, feeling misunderstood and not a little scared. The contractions centered in the small of her back this time, meaning that all afternoon she'd thought she'd had a backache and didn't know she was in labor until her water broke while she was driving home.

"This is Sheriff Pierce. Is Will Wilson still with Daisy? Would you get him for me, please?" Joe gave Jane a thumbs-up sign and she tried to smile.

"So much for matchmaking," she grumbled, lowering herself onto the bed to catch her breath. It seemed to take forever for Will to come to the phone and talk to Joe. They probably interrupted something. Anyone could see by the way those two looked at each other that it wouldn't be long before they did something about it. If other people would just leave them alone long enough.

"Will's coming right over," Joe said, hanging up the phone. "Come on, I'll help you downstairs and I'll give the boys a speech about behaving themselves."

"I wanted him to get married," she said, then tried to pant through the next contraction. "To

Daisy," she said when the pain subsided. "I wanted to have dinner parties."

"Don't get your hopes up," Joe said, helping her stand.

"They're made for each other. Oh, darn, I forgot my shoes!"

"MAKE SURE they go to bed by seven," Jane had panted, one last instruction before a nervous-looking Joe helped her out the door.

"We'll be fine," Will had promised before closing the door.

This wasn't the day he had planned. There'd been no intimate afternoon spent with a naked Daisy, no warm bed and willing woman to look forward to later tonight.

He told himself it was for the best. And he lied.

The two little Pierce boys were easy enough to deal with. They wanted cereal for supper and they were content to watch television and play with a bunch of trucks afterward. Spring, snug in the crib prepared for the new Pierce baby, actually slept for an hour underneath her new quilt. He figured she was all tired out from the baby shower, too. Will collapsed into Joe's leather recliner and watched cartoons while he tried not to fall asleep before the kids went to bed.

He never expected to answer the doorbell and see Daisy standing on the front porch. Snow dusted her blond curls, which she'd released from their usual topknot. She looked tired and smelled like tomato sauce.

"Jane called and asked if I'd mind bringing dinner." She held out a pizza box. "So here it is."

"Come on in," he said, stepping back to let her enter the kitchen. "The kids had cereal, but I wouldn't mind trying your pizza."

"It came out pretty good. I could actually make a profit if this catches on."

Will took the box and inhaled the scent of tomato and oregano. How could he compete with a restaurant? Then he realized what Daisy had said. "Jane called you? In the middle of having a baby?"

"I know, it sounds a little strange," she agreed, looking up at him with those gorgeous blue eyes. "She was panting, so I didn't hear everything she said, but I think I understood enough to bring you something to eat."

"Can you stay?"

"For a little while, I guess." She took off her jacket while he set the pizza on the counter and called for the boys.

"My mom's havin' a baby," Josh announced.

"Yeah," his younger brother said, tucking his hand inside Will's. "A baby."

"I know," Daisy said. "She called me and asked me to bring you a pizza. Would you like some?" Both boys nodded, wide-eyed. Will found plates and silverware, and Daisy served the food to the boys while they wriggled in their seats at the table.

"Your turn," she said, handing him a plate.

"Thanks."

"Be honest," she said.

"About what?"

"Whether it's good or not."

"Sweetheart, it looks almost as good as you."

"Does that line work on cowgirls?"

"Yeah, sometimes."

She rolled her eyes. "You've got to come up with some better lines."

"How about, 'come to bed with me'?"

Daisy laughed, but Will was encouraged. After all, the lady hadn't said no.

SHE WANTED THE COWBOY in her bed. This was lust, pure and simple. An itch that needed to be scratched. Maybe she'd think more clearly about him after she'd made love with him. Had sex with him. Gotten the need for him out of her system in one snowy night.

Half the town already thought she was sleeping with him.

She'd been celibate for two years, five months and twenty-seven days.

As long as she kept from falling in love with him, what could happen? They both knew how to prevent pregnancy and all those nasty diseases. Neither was married.

"Let's get it over with," she said, after Jane's harried sister arrived to take over with the boys, after Will had gathered up Spring and her assorted belongings and walked Daisy out the Pierces' front door into a starlit and snowy night.

"What?"

"Let's get it over with," she repeated. "Do you need to go back to the ranch first? To do, um, ranch things?"

"I left the horses in the barn and Bozeman in the house. I didn't know how late I'd be."

"And I suppose you have a case or two of condoms in the glove compartment of your truck."

"Well, not a case, but—"

"Good. I'll meet you at my house."

She left him standing there, the sleeping baby in his arms, while she walked carefully to her car. This would not be a good time to slip on the ice and fall on her rear end. She didn't look back when she drove away. Instead she concentrated on driving the few short blocks to the restaurant and around the corner to park near her door. She wished she'd left the outside light on to illuminate her path, but there was enough of a moon to relieve the darkness. It was just after eight on a Sunday night, and the small town was as still and quiet as if it was midnight.

Daisy only had time to unlock the door when she saw headlights round the corner and park by the school. She didn't think that would fool anyone, but at least Will had tried to be discreet. He certainly hadn't wasted any time getting here. She took a deep breath and swallowed hard. She was twenty-eight years old and she'd been married twice and she had no reason, no reason at all, to be nervous about this.

Except she would be making love with Will for the first time. And the last.

She wanted a shower. She wanted Spring to sleep for hours. She wanted to open a bottle of wine and smooth over the jagged edges of her nerves.

"I guess this means that you're not interested in Leroy anymore?" He kicked the door shut behind him and bent down to kiss her. A soft kiss, with just a hint of promise, teased her lips before he lifted his head.

"I think he was more interested in my cooking."

"You never said 'let's get it over with' to him?" He looked as if he was going to laugh, but he placed feather-soft kisses beneath her ear and along her jaw.

"No. You're the first."

"How, uh, romantic." Will eased away from her and looked down at the sleeping baby in his arms. "What should we do with our chaperone?"

"I'll fix her a bed on the floor of my room." Which would give her something to do besides disintegrate from nervous energy. Will followed her down the hall to her bedroom, where she stripped the comforter from her bed and folded it into a thick pad for Spring to sleep on. She took the baby from Will's arms and settled her under her quilt.

"I hope this works," she whispered as she stood up.

"Not as much as I do." Will bent down to adjust

the quilt around Spring's shoulders. "The little terror has had a long day. And so have I."

This time she didn't try to ignore the melting feeling she got when she watched him with Spring. "Do you want something to drink?"

"No. Do you?"

Desperately. Especially when he looked at her as if she was a helping of strawberry shortcake. "What happens if I change my mind?"

"We wait 'til tomorrow," he said, taking her hand and guiding her to the bed. "Maybe then you won't look like you're going to the guillotine."

"I don't look like that," she protested, laughing despite her embarrassment.

He tugged her against his chest. "Yes, you do, sweetheart. And as much as I want to toss you into that bed behind you and make love to you for the rest of the night, I'm not going to."

"You're not?" Okay, her world had just come to an end.

"Not until you're sure," he whispered, touching his lips to hers and dropping his hand to the back of her head for one long, sweet kiss before he hesitated, his mouth hovering above hers.

"I absolutely refuse—" she hesitated, feeling him sigh against her mouth "—to have second thoughts."

"That's good news."

Once again she thought she heard him chuckle, but she ran her hands inside his unzipped jacket and along the front of his flannel shirt. He was warmer than she expected, radiating heat and strength and all that wonderful maleness.

"Will?"

"Mmm?"

"Take off your coat." She helped him shove it off his shoulders and toss it to the floor.

"Wait," he said, laughing as he retrieved condoms from his pocket and tossed them onto the bed. "Now it's your turn." He unbuttoned the wooden fasteners that held the edges of the suede together. "You know, I've thought about doing this before. Every time I saw you in this coat."

"You like leather?" She dropped her coat on top of his and kicked them both aside. Heat radiated through her body, intensifying as he kissed her once again.

"I like *you.*" His hands were under her sweater. Hers reached for his shoulders and held on for dear life. His kiss was slow and exploring, as if he had all the time in the world to sample the inside of her mouth. She wanted it to last forever, but if he kissed her like this much longer she'd be on the floor.

Somehow they managed to get their clothes off, though Daisy couldn't remember how. A tangle of arms and legs, kisses and muffled laughter turned into a skin-melting embrace on Daisy's bed. She forgot to be nervous every time his mouth touched hers, she forgot her name as he rained kisses in the valley between her breasts and she forgot to breathe when he took turns teasing each peaked nipple with his lips and tongue.

She didn't want to wait any longer. She wanted him where she knew he belonged tonight, deep inside of her where she ached with the need for him.

"Will," she begged. "Now."

"I thought we had all night," he murmured, but she could tell he was smiling.

"We do." Her hands skimmed his chest, then lower. "But I want you now." Disappointed, she couldn't reach farther than his slim waist and, outlined in the dim light, he moved away from her and found a condom. Then he leaned over her, nudging her legs apart with his knees, his erection smooth and hard against the insides of her thighs. She drew him to her, but he kept himself from entering immediately. Instead, bracing himself on his elbows, he tortured her with a long, bruising kiss while the heat from his body mixed with the moisture from hers, until he eased himself slowly into her. She couldn't believe she was ready for him so quickly, couldn't remember a time when her body had responded this way. He moved inside of her until she was filled, then withdrew, teasing and slow. She whimpered and he slid deeper inside again. Each stroke brought her higher, made her want more. She climaxed almost immediately, tightening around him and moaning softly so as not to wake the child.

Will kissed her neck. And her breasts. And continued to move in her, sweet torture she wanted to last all night long.

The man took his time. As if he was memorizing the feel of her, where to kiss and touch and move to bring her pleasure. She came again when he did, their bodies in tune as if they had been making love to each other for years instead of moments.

Heaven, Daisy decided as the world slowly settled into place, was being in bed with Will Wilson.

SPRING SCREAMED the house down at midnight, waking Daisy and Will with her hunger.

"Her bottle," Daisy moaned. She was wrapped in the warm cocoon of Will's arms, her breasts against his chest and her toes on his shins. He'd never been more comfortable in his life, or more unwilling to leave his bed.

"Yeah," he said, praying for the strength to open his eyes. "I'll do it."

"I'll change her first," Daisy said, slipping out of his arms. "Maybe that will quiet her down."

"You're a good woman." He opened his eyes and caught a tantalizing glimpse of Daisy's bare and luscious bottom before she covered herself with a robe. Her yellow hair spilled around her shoulders and when she bent to retrieve Spring, Will caught a glimpse of cleavage. Those beautiful breasts were enough to make a man glad he was alive.

Speaking of alive, a certain part of his body was standing at attention and hoping the little blonde would shuck the robe and get back into bed. But the tempting vision disappeared down the hall, a screaming baby in her arms. Damn. But then, how long could it take to feed a baby? Will swung his legs over the edge of the bed and looked for his jeans. It took a minute to get them on without hurting himself, but it was possible that Daisy would object to him walking around in his boxers like he owned the place.

"Daisy?"

"What?" She was changing the baby, murmuring nonsense to keep Spring occupied while she put on a clean diaper. She didn't look up.

"I'll fix a bottle," he offered, noticing the cleavage again.

"Okay."

She didn't look up. He wondered if she wanted him to sleep on the couch. Maybe she was having second thoughts about having sex with him. He knew women were different from men, but good sex was good sex and what they'd experienced a few hours ago had been downright phenomenal.

The best he'd ever had. And he'd be willing to bet his last prize money that she'd enjoyed it as much as he had. Will padded out to the kitchen and found the diaper bag on the table. Pretty soon he'd opened a new can of formula and filled four plastic bottles. Three he put in the refrigerator and the other he ran under hot tap water. Spring was starting to rev up her lungs again, so Will hurried to test the milk and then brought it in to Daisy.

Who wasn't there.

She was propped up in her bed with all of the pillows behind her back and neck, the baby cradled in her arms, the covers a jumble around her feet. Will knelt on the bed and leaned over to hand her the bottle.

"Say 'thank you, Uncle Will,'" she told the baby, and then smiled at Will as Spring latched on to the bottle and sucked furiously. "She has your appetite."

"And her mother's temper," he added, sitting on the bed beside them.

"I wonder if Jane's had the baby yet."

"I could call the hospital."

She shook her head and popped the nipple out of Spring's mouth. The baby grimaced, but within seconds of being held upright and patted, she burped. "We'll let Joe tell us in the morning. I hope it's a girl," she said, giving Spring the rest of her midnight supper.

"A quiet girl," Will joked while watching the tender expression on Daisy's face as she fed the baby. She was getting fond of Spring, that was clear, but what would happen after Sarah returned? He would be free to nail a For Sale sign on the fence. And Daisy would be free of them both.

He hated that idea.

"Give her to me," he said when Spring finished her bottle. "I'll put her down."

"She fell asleep without burping."

"That's okay. She does that sometimes." He padded across the room and laid the baby down without waking her. He had other things on his mind besides babies and bottles and burping. He shut off the lights in the kitchen and living room before hurrying back to Daisy's bedroom. She propped herself up on one elbow and watched him remove his jeans.

He hesitated before standing naked and partially aroused in front of her. "What are you looking at?" Which was an unnecessary question, considering the direction of her gaze.

"You," she said. "You're so comfortable with all of this."

"This?" He slid under the covers and Daisy rearranged the pillows so he had a couple under his head. He shifted so his erection didn't touch her thigh.

"Sex," she explained, leaning over so she could look into his face. The sheet was securely fastened around her bosom, tempting Will to give the fabric a little tug. "You're just so comfortable with this one-night stand business."

One night? He tugged a little harder on the sheet and watched the material slip lower, stopping just short of revealing a pair of enticing nipples. "Meaning that the thousands of women I've slept with have made me easy with this lovemaking business?"

"Thousands?" She leaned closer, her lips curved into a mischievous smile, and the tip of one breast grazed his upper arm. "That's all?"

He tugged the sheet free and pulled her on top of him. "Dunno," he said, his voice thickening as she settled between his thighs. "Millions, maybe."

"Ah," she said, kissing the side of his mouth. "I thought so."

"But you're the first—honey, don't move like that or this will all be over in a matter of seconds."

She wriggled against him anyway. "You mean a man of your experience can't control himself?"

He lifted her off him and reached for another condom while she unwound the tangle of sheets from her legs. "Sweetheart, come here and do that again."

"I get to be on top?"

"For a while," he said, positioning that beautiful body over his. "Until I get bored."

Daisy laughed, and lowered herself onto him in a tantalizingly slow motion that made him grit his teeth and try not to groan aloud. If Spring woke now, Will figured he'd probably expire of frustration. Daisy teased him, riding him slowly with deep thrusts. She clearly enjoyed taking her time.

"Bored yet?"

"Nope." He captured one breast and laved the nipple, then paid equal attention to the other. "Are you?"

"Mmm, oh, no, don't stop," she moaned, riding him harder. He gripped her hips and urged her on, until she tightened and climaxed around him. He felt the tiny contractions as she collapsed on top of him.

"Sweetheart," he whispered into her ear.

"Mmm?"

"My turn to be on top." He rolled her over, staying deep within her, and slowly rode her until she climaxed again, and so did he, sensation after mind-blowing sensation beating in rhythm with his heart.

HE LEFT while she was in the shower. Daisy, hair dripping into the collar of her robe, entered her bedroom and saw that his clothes were gone. And so was Spring, and her new quilt. The house was silent and empty and horrible.

She should have known. There would be no embarrassing morning scenes, no stilted conversations, no empty promises like "I'll call you later" to remind her that she had spent the night with a man she barely knew.

But she liked him. A lot. And maybe—just maybe—she was a little bit in love with him. No one could blame her. Will Wilson had enough charm for three men. And when he walked into the café with that sweet infant in his arms, well, Daisy had seen more than one woman's head swivel in his direction. Surely she couldn't be criticized for inviting him into her bed.

She dressed quickly, conscious of the tender areas of her body that reminded her of last night. She'd slept like a dead woman in between lovemaking. She'd heard Will out in the kitchen this morning when she woke, but she'd hurried into the bathroom for a shower before greeting him. One glance in the bathroom mirror told her she'd made the right move.

Daisy went into the kitchen and noticed that Will had made a pot of coffee. He must do that for all his lovers, she thought. A nice gesture for a worn-out woman the morning after.

She sipped her coffee and eyed the cold gray light of dawn out the kitchen window. Last night had been an experience. One she wouldn't soon forget.

It was time to get to work. And back to celibacy.

11

"WHAT ARE YOU DOING in town so early?" Joe shut the door of his truck and motioned for Will to follow him into the house. Will unhooked Spring from her car seat and bundled her into a blanket before crossing the yard. Joe held the door open for him.

"Thanks." He didn't answer the question. He and Joe had been the only two people driving through Main Street this morning and Will couldn't leave Cowman's Corner without knowing about the Pierces' new child.

"So, did you have a boy or a girl?"

Joe broke into a wide grin. "A girl. Hannah Jane. Eight pounds, ten ounces. Healthy as a horse, too."

Will shook his friend's hand. "Congratulations. That's great. How's Jane?"

"Tired, but ready to go out and buy all sorts of pink outfits." He took off his coat and tossed it over the back of the sofa. "Bring the baby and come on in the kitchen. I'll make us a pot of coffee."

"Sounds good," Will said, thinking as he followed Joe that a cup of coffee would probably save his life. He wanted to lie down on the kitchen floor and die.

"Late night?"

Will fingered his day-old beard and grimaced. "I guess neither one of us would win any beauty contests this morning. What are you doing home?"

"Jane wanted me to be here when the boys woke up. I'm going to tell them they have a baby sister and get them off to school before I head to the office for a while. I'll go back to the hospital this afternoon and then tomorrow Jane and the baby come home."

"That's fast."

"That's the way they do it now." Joe filled the coffeepot and turned on the switch. "So, do I ask why you were driving through town at five-thirty this morning? You were the last person I expected to see when I came home."

"You'd better not ask."

"Meaning you spent the night with a lady." Joe leaned against the counter and crossed his arms in front of his chest.

Will sat down on a kitchen chair and unwrapped the baby, who looked at him with curious blue eyes. "Meaning I'd better not say."

"Jane was wrong, then."

"About what?"

Joe laughed and turned to get mugs from the cupboard. He poured two cups of coffee and set one on the table by Will. "She thought baby-sitting for the boys would keep you determined to stay single."

"I like the boys," Will said, remembering how funny those two little kids were with the stringy pizza cheese. "And I like being single, too."

"Yeah. That's what I told her."

Will looked down at Spring, who lay comfortably against his shoulder. "I'm gonna miss her, though."

Joe sat down and took a sip of coffee. "Why? Are you going somewhere?"

"Not yet. But I'm going to call that private detective again and see if he can scare up anything else about Sarah. And you have the truck. We're getting close." He picked up his coffee and drank. "Don't give me that look like you're feeling sorry for me."

"Why would I feel sorry for you? You've inherited a ranch. You own three of the best quarter horses in the country, you've got a pile of money invested in God knows what—"

"Something about the Internet," Will said, not knowing much more than that.

"And you spent the night with—well, anyway, you know what I mean. Your life isn't exactly going to hell in a hay cart."

Will was silent for a minute while he thought that over. "How'd you know that Jane was the woman you wanted to marry?"

Joe grinned. "I saw her and I knew."

"Just like that?"

He nodded. "Yeah. Just like that. Just like a bolt of lightning on a hot summer night."

"That was easy enough." Almost as easy as falling into bed with Daisy.

"Yeah," Joe said. "The hard part was convincing her to marry me. She wasn't exactly hit by lightning when she saw me."

"No kidding?"

"Why the questions? Are you thinking about settling down?"

Will stalled and took another gulp of hot coffee, letting the liquid burn his throat on the way down to his gut. Thinking about marriage? No, he was thinking about making love to Daisy for a few years or so, wondering what it would be like to know she was his, hoping that he would see her later on today and fighting the urge to return to her house and beg to be admitted so he could crawl back in that soft, warm bed and make love to her a few more times before lunch. Will glanced down at the baby as she made a noise in his arms. "Me? Settle down? Hell, no."

Little Spring stared up at him as if she knew he was the biggest liar in all of Montana.

He sure hoped she didn't inherit the Wilson sex drive.

"WELL, HOW WAS IT?"

"How was what?" Daisy tried to move out of Heather's way, but the young woman had her cornered by the coffeemaker. She really hoped Heather wasn't asking what she thought she was asking.

"A certain rodeo champ was seen driving away from your house this morning," Heather reported, thankfully keeping her voice low. "Way to go, Daize!"

"Maybe I should fire you."

Heather shrugged, completely unperturbed by

the threat. "Then you'd be stuck here all the time," she pointed out. "With no time for cowboys."

"I'm not admitting anything."

"You don't have to, Daisy. Sexual satisfaction is written all over your face." Heather giggled and let Daisy pass with the coffee carafe.

What was written all over her face was exhaustion, Daisy decided, ignoring Leroy Doyle, who was waving his empty coffee mug. It was only nine o'clock in the morning, but already it felt like twelve hours later. She just wasn't used to that much nighttime exercise, she figured. From now on she'd get a good night's sleep—alone, of course—but she'd never forget last night.

"What are you smiling at?"

Daisy almost bumped into Barlow, who popped out of the storeroom with an armload of paper towels. "Nothing."

He gave her a knowing look as he passed, but fortunately didn't say anything. Daisy wondered if Heather had told him anything. Well, she could deny it. And she was the boss, so she could forbid anyone to talk about it.

She hoped.

Before she took a tea break, she stopped at the lunch counter and refilled coffee cups. "Has anyone heard if the Pierces had their baby last night?"

No one had.

"Call the sheriff's office," one of the men suggested. "The dispatcher should know where he is."

"You don't hafta," Leroy said. "His truck just pulled up out front."

One of the others craned his neck to peer out the front window. "And Billy Wilson's right behind him."

"Goody," Heather said, slipping past Daisy to place an order with Barlow. "Three over easy with the works!"

She'd hoped he'd have the sense to stay away, but she should have known better. She didn't want to see him.

She did want to see him. It was just that the last time she'd gazed into those sexy eyes of his, he'd been rolling off her naked body. He'd kissed her before she fell asleep, one satisfied and weary woman. She would pretend nothing happened, she decided, filling the empty carafe with water for a new pot of coffee.

"It's a girl," Joe announced over the jingle of the bell above the door.

There was a flood of congratulations, back-pounding, handshaking and some general teasing about the difficulty of raising a daughter.

"Wouldn't trade my Darla for anything," Charlie declared, motioning Joe and Will to stools just vacated. "Girls take care of you in your old age."

"No kidding?" Will sat down and pushed dirty dishes out of his way, which prompted Daisy to pick up a damp rag and clean off the counter in front of him.

"Good morning," she said, hoping she sounded

professional. She cleared six feet of dishes, then wiped off the counter. She made sure she didn't touch him. "Coffee?"

"Yes," he said, smiling at her. "Please."

"Joe?"

"Definitely, thanks." The sheriff smiled at her, too. "I heard you brought over pizza last night. The boys got a real kick out of that."

"They're cute kids," she said, glad of the excuse to avoid Will's gaze as she set coffee mugs in front of them and turned around for the carafe. "Congratulations on the baby girl. How's Jane doing?"

"She's tired, but happy."

Daisy carefully filled the cups and returned the carafe. "When was the baby born?"

"Shortly after midnight. It sure didn't take long." He shook his head. "Jane was a real trouper."

Daisy thought briefly of what she and Will were doing "shortly after midnight" and she blushed. She hoped the men would assume it was the heat from the kitchen, but Will looked at her and winked.

She ignored him and pulled out an order pad. "What'll you have?"

"Hotcakes and eggs," Joe said.

"Make that two," Will added. "I've got a ferocious appetite this morning."

Daisy ignored him and took her sweet time writing up the order. "Fine," she said, and instead of posting the order at the window, hurried into the kitchen to hide.

Barlow shot her an odd look. "What's the matter with you?"

"Nothing. I'm going to fix a cup of tea. Do you want one?"

"Sure. Herbal."

"Once a hippie, always a hippie," she said, quoting one of Barlow's favorite lines. "How are the dogs?"

"Well, there are still too many of them," he said. "I spend a fortune on—hey, where are you going?"

Daisy didn't take time to reply. She rounded the corner and stopped in front of Will. She'd been too tired to realize something—someone—was missing. "Where's Spring?"

He set down his coffee cup. "Do you think I lost her?"

"Don't tease. Is she—" She couldn't say "with her mother." The words wouldn't form.

Joe intervened. "She's with my sister-in-law. Judy said she'd stay with her while she took her morning nap in Hannah's crib."

"Oh. Well..."

"Did you think I left her in the truck?" Will didn't sound too happy. "I drove out to the farm to check on the animals and, uh, clean up. Work goes faster without Spring around."

"Yes," Daisy said.

"And Joe's going to be making phone calls about Sarah's truck," he added. "I thought I'd stick around town for a while and see what turns up."

For a cowboy, he didn't spend a lot of time on his ranch. "Oh."

"Are you making pizza again tonight?"

Daisy wondered if that's what he was really asking. "I'm not sure," she stammered, and looked at her watch. "Excuse me," she said. "I have to, uh, make a phone call."

She hurried back to the kitchen and leaned against the wall, out of sight of the customers at the counter.

"What's the matter with you?" Barlow flipped another hotcake in the air and it fell neatly to the grill. "Your order's almost up."

"I need willpower," she said. "Buckets of it."

"Why? Just because you slept with Billy?"

Her heart fell to the thick soles of her extra-support shoes. "Heather told you?"

"No, Bonnie was out walking the dogs this morning and saw his truck parked near your house. She put two and two together."

"Do you think the whole town knows?"

"Not yet." He flipped the hotcakes onto a plate and turned to grin at her. "But they will. Maude Anderson gets up early and her second-floor bedroom looks out on the school."

"How would you know that?"

"I painted it for her a few years ago." He fixed another plate of eggs and hotcakes and set them on the counter. "There is nothing you can do in this town without everyone knowing about it, Daisy."

She groaned. "Maude thinks he's married. She'll

tell everyone that I'm a, uh, wanton woman and no one will let their husbands eat here again."

Barlow grinned. "No way, Daize. They'll figure Billy Wilson will spoil you for anyone else."

She crossed the room and grabbed the plates. "I'll act like nothing happened," she muttered. "And they can all think what they want."

Daisy left the kitchen with her chin in the air.

HE COULDN'T FIGURE OUT what the hell was wrong with her. Last Friday she'd been loving and warm, a willing woman in his arms for one long, incredibly passionate night. Then all weekend she'd ignored him. Now it was Monday and he still felt like he was a stranger to Daisy again. Damn women. They shouldn't be this hard to understand. Will put his feet up on the sheriff's desk and tilted back in his chair. Surely Joe had to come back eventually.

He watched Spring, asleep in her car seat in a draft-free corner of the office. With any luck they'd find her mother this week. Maybe even today, if the police computer systems were all they were cracked up to be.

Daisy didn't serve him breakfast this morning. Instead he'd had to tease Heather and make conversation about the weather with the guys lined up on stools at the counter. Daisy hadn't even come over to refill his coffee or to heat up Spring's bottle.

He hated that.

When Joe came in, Will removed his boots from

the top of the desk and put all four of the chair legs on the floor. "Anything?"

"The truck was registered to a Steve Whelan, in Las Vegas. We're trying to reach him now." Joe hung up his hat and coat on the rack behind the door.

"I can fly there this morning," Will said. If this Steve Whelan had hurt Sarah, he'd pay.

"You're going to stay out of it until we know what's going on," Joe said, moving a pile of files off the seat of his chair so he could sit down. "The truck could be stolen."

"Sarah wouldn't steal."

"You haven't seen her in years, Will. You don't know what she's capable of now."

He didn't want to believe that. His little sister had been sweet and kind and shy. "She's no criminal."

"When I need you to go to Vegas or anywhere else, I'll tell you," Joe promised. "Until then, stay put. I don't think our little mother is too far away."

"Why not?"

Joe shrugged. "Just a hunch. It's only been eight days."

"She could have hitchhiked to Alaska by now."

"Maybe. Maybe not." Joe leaned forward. "For now, your job is to take care of that baby. And get yourself a lawyer."

"Why?"

"Sooner or later someone is going to come back for that little girl, Will. You'd better be prepared. I know you don't want to believe it, but if this baby isn't Sarah's you could be facing a paternity suit."

"She's not mine," Will said, looking over at the sleeping child. But sometimes, just sometimes, he wished like hell that she was.

Fatherhood wasn't so bad.

DAISY STRUGGLED to cross the Pierces' front lawn. Between the north wind and the layer of ice coating the dry grass, she had a heck of a time not falling on her face. Or on the six boxes of pizza she carried in her arms. She made it to the front porch, though, and managed to ring the bell with her left elbow.

Joe opened it almost immediately. "Daisy? Come on in."

"I called," she said. "Jane said it was okay to come over and see the baby."

"She told me. Here, let me help you with those." He lifted the boxes out of her arms and held the door open. The television blasted from one corner and Jane sat in a rocking chair with a tiny bundle of pink blanket in her arms.

"Thanks. I thought they might come in handy."

He gave her a blank look.

"I made pizza and froze them for you. I thought some easy dinners would help Jane."

"You are an angel," Jane called from across the room. She clicked the remote control and the room became silent. "Joe, would you put those—all but one—in the freezer?"

"Sure. Thanks again, Daisy. That was real nice of you," he said, but he gave his wife an odd look.

Daisy hesitated before taking off her coat. "Are you sure you want company?"

"I called you, didn't I? I wanted you to meet Hannah." Jane held up the baby. A tiny pink face topped by dark hair peeked out of the blanket. "Want to hold her?"

"I'd love to." She took the baby in her arms and sat down on the nearby sofa. "She's so little."

"She's bigger than the boys were when they were born, but—" The doorbell rang, interrupting Jane's words. "Daisy, would you mind getting that? Joe's in the basement."

"Sure." But the smile on Jane's face as Daisy returned the baby to her made Daisy suspect that Jane knew who she'd see on the other side of the door.

The cowboy stood on the doorstep, the baby bundled in his arms. He shivered as she stared at him. "Are you going to let us in?"

Daisy stepped back.

"I didn't know you were going to be here," she said.

"You've been avoiding us." He looked past Daisy. "Hi, Jane. Is that the new kid?"

"A playmate for Spring," she said. "Come see."

Joe stuck his head out of the kitchen. "Will?"

"Yeah. I got your message. What's up?"

The sheriff glanced at his wife. "Maybe you'd better ask Jane."

"Maybe you'd better open some beer or wine or

something," she suggested. "I think we're having a party."

"We are?"

"I can't stay," Daisy said, looking at her watch and pretending seven-thirty on a Thursday night was past her bedtime. Will came over and sat beside her on the couch. He handed her Spring.

"She's missed you," he said.

"I've been busy." Daisy felt incredibly foolish. What on earth was she afraid of? Stripping off her clothes and making love to him on the Pierces' braided rug? "Hi, sweetie," she said to Spring. "How's life on the ranch?"

Joe leaned in the doorway. "Beer or wine, Will?"

"Beer for me."

Joe looked at Daisy. "Beer, wine, soda pop, coffee?"

"Go ahead," Jane urged. "Have a glass of wine with me. The doctor swears it's good for nursing mothers, so we splurged on the expensive stuff."

"Okay," she agreed.

"Come out and see it," Will said.

"See what?"

"The ranch. I've been working on the house."

"Getting it ready to sell?" And why should she care if he sold the place? It was none of her concern. One night of incredibly wonderful lovemaking did not mean that she needed to be interested in the real-estate part of his life.

"Yeah." But he didn't smile. "You'd see a big difference."

Jane excused herself, mumbling something about changing Hannah's diaper, and disappeared from the room.

"You've been avoiding me," Will said. "Why?"

"So what happened last week won't happen again."

"It was that bad?"

"It was that good."

"Sweetheart," he said, running his index finger down her cheek to the tip of her chin and turning her to face him. "You're making me crazy."

And now she *was* in danger of ripping off her clothes and making love to him on the faded braided rug. Thank goodness she was holding Spring. Daisy took a deep breath. "People are talking."

His head dipped lower. "The story of my life, honey."

"And they think you're married."

His lips brushed hers. "Come home with me tonight. Tomorrow you can tell everyone I got a divorce."

"And the baby?"

"Spring has a new crib, remember?"

"That's not what I—"

He kissed her then, a long, deep kiss that promised all sorts of glorious hours in the night ahead. And Daisy forgot every resolution she'd ever made.

JOE LOCKED the front door and turned off the porch light before turning to his beaming wife. "Nice work."

"Thank you."

"You planned the whole thing, getting them both to come over here at the same time?"

"Yes, sir, I certainly did." She smiled as he crossed the room and bent down over her rocking chair. Hannah was asleep at her breast. "That isn't against the law, is it?"

"Men don't have a chance, do they?"

She shook her head. "Nope."

Joe, careful not to wake the sleeping baby, kissed his wife. "You really think Will is going to stick around this town?"

"He's a fool if he doesn't," Jane declared. "But no one ever said that men were smart."

"I was," her adoring husband said. And kissed her again.

WILL UNDRESSED DAISY with gentle precision, revealing each inch of pale peach skin in slow motion. He nibbled his way along her collarbone, lingered at her breasts until he was dizzy with needing her, then moved lower. After long minutes she stood naked, shivering a little in the cool first-floor room that served as a bedroom.

"Come to bed," Will said, barely able to speak. Could he have forgotten how beautiful this woman was?

"I thought that one night would be enough," Daisy said, shaking her head as if she was laughing at herself. She slipped inside the sheets and pulled the covers up to her chin. Still fully dressed, Will sat on the edge of the bed and tucked a silky strand of hair behind her ear.

"You were wrong." He smiled and began to unbutton his shirt.

"I don't know what we're doing," she confessed. "But I'm glad we're out here at the ranch where no one can see my car parked in the yard."

"How long can you stay?"

She smiled, a lazy seductive smile that made him ache and harden against his jeans. "Until I get bored."

Will was out of his clothes in nine seconds. Two seconds later he was beside her in the bed. And about two hours later, sated and sleepy, he withdrew from her warm body and held her against him.

He should have gone to sleep—he was definitely tired enough—but something was nagging at him. "Daisy," he whispered. "Daisy?"

"Um?"

"Nothing," he said, kissing her forehead. "Go back to sleep."

He'd wanted to ask her why she came home with him tonight. If she cared about him. And about Spring. Or if she only needed a warm body beside hers once in a while to kill the loneliness.

Tomorrow, he decided. Tomorrow there would be time for answers.

12

"STAY," he said, reaching for her hand as she started to scoot off the bed.

"I can't." But Daisy sank down onto the mattress and turned her back on the window with its view of a rapidly lightening sky. "I'm going to be late for work."

"Barlow and what's-her-name can handle it."

"Barlow and Heather will need help."

"You work too hard," he grumbled, nuzzling her neck and making it hard for her to leave the bed.

"And you don't work at all."

"I'm in between jobs," he pointed out, kissing the valley between her breasts. "Maybe I'll stay here and become a rancher."

And maybe daffodils would bloom in January. "Uh-huh," Daisy said, laughing as she moved away from him.

He frowned. "You think that's funny? I'm giving it some heavy-duty thought, sweetheart."

"And I suppose you'll join the chamber of commerce and the Boosters Club, too." She tugged the sheet loose so she could wrap it around her, and tiptoed across the room to the crib. Spring was sleeping deeply, her tiny fist curled near her mouth as if she wanted to suck her thumb.

"I'm going to keep her," he said, and this time Daisy heard the serious note in his voice.

She turned away from the baby and faced the man she'd made love with most of the night. "How?"

"I'll move into town. Hire a housekeeper."

It was none of her business, and not her job to point out that raising a child wasn't that easy. Or how expensive. Besides, maybe rodeo champions made more money than she thought. "And what about her mother?"

"She'll have one," he said, not taking his gaze from her face. "I'm thinking about getting married."

Daisy stared at him. She would have given a week's worth of business income to know what he was thinking behind that inscrutable expression. "Oh?"

"She bosses me around something awful," he continued. "But I think she—"

The ringing of the phone interrupted his words. Will reached down and grabbed the portable phone from the floor beside the bed. "Hello?" The color drained from his face. "Don't let her out of your sight. Yeah, right away."

Daisy waited, forcing herself to stand there and wait for Will to explain. He clicked off the phone and looked over at her as if she were a stranger.

"That was Joe, calling from the office. She's here," he announced.

"Who?" But even as she asked the question she knew what the answer would be.

"Spring's mother. Sarah's come home."

WILL DIDN'T RECOGNIZE her at first. He'd expected a run-down, scared waif, but the person he saw in Joe's office was a sturdy young woman who was a lot taller than he remembered. Her clothes looked worn and faded, though clean, and her light brown hair hung down her back in a long braid. But the forlorn look on her face broke his heart.

"Sarah?"

"Willie?"

He took her in his arms and fought back the emotions that threatened to overwhelm him. "Hey, kid, I've missed you." He heard the gruffness of his voice and hoped he didn't sound as if he was going to cry. He wouldn't want her to think he'd gotten soft in his middle age.

"Me, too," she sniffed, hugging him close to her. "I'm sorry, I really really am."

"It's okay," he said, letting her sob against his chest. "Everything's going to be okay now."

"I knew you'd take good care of her. The sheriff said Rebecca was doing fine," she said, taking deep gulps of air as she pulled away from him.

"Rebecca, huh? It would have been nice if you'd put her name in the note you left."

"You must hate me."

"Hate you?" He relented and tweaked her braid,

a long familiar way to tease her. "Not in a million years."

"Where is she?"

"With a friend. We'll go get her in a few minutes, but first we have to talk." He led her over to a chair. "You're going to tell me everything."

Sarah's eyes filled with tears again. "Mom would kill me."

"Mom would want her granddaughter to be taken care of," he reminded her. "Not dumped on the front porch on the ranch, Sarah."

"I wanted to come in," she whispered. "I planned to, 'til I stood on the porch. I thought I was going to throw up, because I hated that house so much and I knew I couldn't go inside. And I was so ashamed of everything."

Will hardened his heart to the new tears streaming down his sister's cheeks and pulled a chair over to face her. "Now," he said. "Start from the beginning, honey. You've sure got some explaining to do."

"WHOA," Heather said, her pencil poised above her order pad as she stared at her boss. "What the heck—"

"Never mind," Daisy said, carrying the car seat and Spring toward the kitchen. The café, crowded with customers at six-thirty in the morning, quieted to a low murmur of conversation, but Daisy ignored the curious stares directed her way. "Do me a favor,

Heather, and bring me a cup of tea and some breakfast."

"Like what?"

"Anything Barlow can make fast," she said, heading across the room to the back. She didn't even know why she'd come in through the front door, except that she needed to talk to Heather and see how business was. Now she'd given the folks in town something to talk about.

They'd have plenty more to talk about by lunchtime. She managed to rest the car seat on her hip while she unlocked the door, then made her way to the living room.

"You poor thing, shifted around like a sack of potatoes all the time." Daisy lifted car seat and baby over to her sofa, then sat down beside them in the quiet of her apartment. She should be helping Heather with the breakfast rush, but there was no way she was going to leave Spring.

Her mother would come for her soon enough, and then what would Daisy do? Go back to work, she told herself. There was a stack of paperwork on the coffee table in front of her, things that needed to be recorded for taxes. She had a business; she had a life.

And she was in love.

Which didn't mean anyone—especially Will—would have to know. Unless he loved her, too, which Daisy knew was more than a little farfetched. She unfastened Spring's safety straps and lifted the baby into her lap. She balanced her on her knees and tickled the little girl's chin. "Your Uncle Will is a no-good cowboy," she told her. "But he sure took good care of you, didn't he?"

Spring almost smiled.

"Your mommy's coming," she whispered. "I'll bet she's missed you."

"Daisy?"

Heather opened the hall door and poked her head in. "I have your breakfast."

"Great." Daisy tucked the baby back into her car seat, which made Spring frown. "I'll fix you in a minute," she promised, and took a plate full of scrambled eggs and toast in one hand and a mug of tea in the other from Heather.

"Nice place," she said, looking around at the overstuffed chintz furniture. "Real cozy."

"Thanks. Holler if you need me, but—" She attempted a smile. "Try not to need me."

"Sure thing." Heather paused. "Are you okay? Did Billy dump you already?"

Great. She looked like she'd been dumped? "Spring's mother is back."

"Oh." Heather glanced toward the baby and then to Daisy. "Is he really married like you said?"

"It's complicated," Daisy said, moving toward the kitchen. "Thanks for breakfast."

"No problem." Heather reached into her apron pocket and unwrapped a stick of gum. "I'll bet a woman gets hungry after she's been having sex with Billy Wilson all night."

THREE HOURS LATER he came to get the baby. He and an attractive, young—very young—woman entered the restaurant and headed toward Daisy, who had been putting a new tape in the cash register. So this was Spring's mother.

"Daisy, I'd like you to meet my sister. Sarah," Will said, turning to a young woman who had Will's eyes. "This is Daisy, the friend who's helped me with, uh, Rebecca."

"Rebecca?"

"That was her name," Sarah said. "But Will said he named her Spring." She looked around the restaurant. "I like that better. Is she here?"

"The cook just took her," Daisy said, wondering how this pale young woman could think she was old enough to take care of a baby. "She likes walks around the kitchen. I think the shiny pans..." Her voice trailed off as she realized that no one was really listening to a word she babbled.

"Well, it sure is nice to meet you." Sarah glanced nervously toward the kitchen.

Daisy looked at Will, hoping for some clue as to what was going on. Was he going to return the baby as if nothing had happened? Will didn't meet her gaze, instead he clapped his hand on his sister's shoulder. "Let's go see her, Sarah."

She took a deep breath and looked at him with wide eyes. "Okay."

"How about if I get her and you meet me in the apartment?" Daisy pulled the key out of her pocket and gave it to Will. "It's a little more private."

"Good idea." He ushered his sister toward the back room as Maude Anderson waved furiously from the corner booth.

"Is that her?" she hissed, scooting over to Daisy. "The crazy wife?"

"That's his sister," Daisy said, hoping she sounded calm and in control. "There wasn't any wife."

Maude smiled and patted her arm. "I didn't think there was, honey." She winked. "Not yet, anyway."

"You'll have to excuse me." Daisy tried to look like she was having a normal day, as if the lunch crowd wasn't listening to every word that was spoken. As if the man she was in love with hadn't said he was thinking about getting married and given her a look that would melt chocolate.

And who didn't need her anymore.

"GIVING HER THAT BABY was the hardest thing I've ever done in my whole life," Daisy said. Then she sniffed. Jane passed her a box of tissues across the table. "Even worse than finding Johnny in bed with that rodeo queen. Or when Ed took off with—well, never mind. I should know better by now."

Jane would have loved to have heard what husband number two did—and with whom—but she resisted asking. For now. She waited for Daisy to finish blowing her nose before she asked, "And what did Will do?"

"He just stood there. He made her take that baby,

as if he couldn't wait to leave. As if he couldn't wait to be free again."

"Are you sure?"

"Yesterday morning he looked at me and told me that he was thinking about getting married. Yesterday afternoon he couldn't even look me in the eye."

Jane almost dropped Hannah. "He *what?*"

"When a man's naked, in bed, and he's talking about marriage, would you assume he's on the verge of proposing?"

Now that was a good question. She readjusted the baby and took another sip of coffee. "I haven't had a lot of experience in that department, Daisy. But for Will to even say the word *marriage* there had to be something to it. What did you do?"

"Nothing. I thought my heart had stopped. I wasn't even sure I'd heard right."

"And then?"

"And then the phone rang, Joe calling to say Sarah was in town."

"I guess she was trying to hitchhike out to the ranch, but one of the deputies saw her and gave her a ride to town," Jane explained. "I've never seen Joe get dressed that fast in my life."

"She's so young, Jane." Daisy blew her nose. "Sweet and pretty, but very young. I keep wondering how she'll manage."

"I guess she'll stay with Will out at the ranch. And maybe we can both help her out with the baby, teach her how to be a good mother." Jane lifted Hannah to her shoulder and patted her little back. "And then when things settle down a little, you and Will can start, uh, seeing each other again."

"We weren't exactly dating, Jane. It was only one of those 'good sex' kind of things."

"Well, thank goodness for good sex." Jane laughed. "You're blushing."

"I practically dragged him into bed with me," she admitted.

"You're in love with him."

Daisy shook her head. "Nope. Not any more."

Jane reached over and patted her hand. "This can all work out. Just give it time."

Daisy managed a watery smile. "Time? There's no such thing. Barlow told me today he heard that Will's selling the ranch." She took a deep breath. "Which is a good thing. The sooner he leaves town the better."

"Are you sure?"

"I'm sure. I am never making a mistake like this again. How hard could it be to find a nice, pleasant, reliable man who wants to have a couple of kids?"

Jane winced. "From what I hear on the talk shows, you'd think it was just about impossible."

Daisy sniffed. "Well, if all else fails, there's always artificial insemination."

"SHE BARELY SPOKE to me," Will complained. Joe took two beers from the bartender and handed one to Will.

"And you were expecting—?"

Will shrugged. "I thought she'd say something. Anything. I go there for breakfast and she puts a plate of eggs in front of me and tells me to have a nice day like I'm some stranger passing through. I go there for lunch and she talks about the weather. I order pizza at night and she's talking to Leroy Doyle."

"And what about Sarah? How's she doing?"

"She cries a lot. And she spends a lot of time on the phone. I took her into North Bend to talk to some therapist." He ran his hand through his hair. "She stopped crying after that, but she's been here for two weeks. Two long weeks." Two long weeks without being able to be with Daisy. Two long weeks sleeping with Bozeman. He picked up his beer without drinking it. "Did you bring the papers?"

"Are you sure you want to do this?" Joe took a thick wad of papers out of the inside pocket of his jacket and set them on the bar. "It's not too late to change your mind."

"I'm not changing my mind, Joe." He picked up the papers. "This is my copy?"

"You need to read them so we can make the changes tomorrow."

Will tucked them in his jacket. "I'm sure there won't be any. The sooner I get out of that place, the better." He finished the beer and stood.

Joe nodded toward a couple of young women who couldn't stop looking at the rodeo star. "You're not staying?"

Will barely noticed them. "No. Maybe I'll drive by Daisy's apartment and see if the light's on."

"Good luck."

"Thanks," he muttered, remembering once more how she'd felt beneath him. Warm and smooth, wet and slick. "I need all the luck I can get," he admitted, looking around the room at the assortment of people dancing to Garth Brooks on the jukebox. "I'm getting too old for this bar shit."

"A piece of advice? Leave Daisy alone unless you love her," Joe said. He set a ten on the bar and got off the stool. "And don't let her go if you do."

Which, Will thought glumly, was easier said than done. And he said so.

"Jeez, Will, don't you know what it is you want by now?" Joe walked with him out the door and into the parking lot.

He looked up at the stars and took deep breaths of cold Montana air. All he wanted to do was be with Daisy. But forever? Somehow that didn't seem so gut-twistingly scary. "I guess I'd better go home and start figuring it out."

"HE'S HERE and he wants to see you," Heather said, sticking her head into the kitchen. "I don't think he's going to go—what the heck's the matter?"

"Barlow slipped while taking out the trash." She put a dish towel full of ice on the cook's right wrist. "How's that?"

"Better," he said, looking over her shoulder. "My eggs are burning."

"Oh, right." She grabbed a spatula and flipped the eggs onto a plate. "Who are these for?"

"Me," Barlow said. "Thought I'd eat before the lunch business started."

"Can you eat with your left hand?" She held out a fork.

"Sure. Quit fussing, I'm fine. Nothing's broken," he said, taking the plate with his free hand. "Your boyfriend's here."

"I heard. He can wait."

Barlow grinned. "I don't think so. He's right behind you. Hey, Billy."

"Hey, Barlow, how's it goin'?"

Daisy spun around. "You can't come back into the kitchen," was the only thing she could think of to say. He looked so darn handsome standing there, even though he lacked his usual cocky smile.

"Have a nice day. It feels like snow again. I'll be with you in a minute, after I ring up Leroy's order."

"What?"

"That's all you ever say to me," Will told her. "For the past two weeks you've treated me like a stranger."

"I thought it was for the best," she explained. "I thought that was what you wanted."

"What I wanted," he said, taking two steps to bring him within touching distance. He lowered his voice. "What I wanted was you."

Ah, sex again. Oh, it was so tempting. She looked back at Barlow, who winked, and then up at Will. "Could we talk about this later on tonight? I have work to—"

"Nope." With a single, effortless motion he swung her into his arms. "I thought you might marry me instead."

She lifted her chin. "I'm not that desperate."

"Daisy!" Heather screeched from behind Will. "Are you out of your mind? He's asking you to marry him. There aren't that many single men in town, remember?"

Will tightened his grip and spun toward the dining area. "Barlow, why don't you see a doctor? And

Heather? Put the Closed sign on the door, lock it up and take the rest of the day off."

"Cool."

Daisy decided it was time she said something intelligent and commanding, but Will's hand under her thigh crept higher and cut off her will to speak. Barlow and Heather took her silence as a sign of agreement and did exactly what Will had suggested.

"Which way—back door or through the restaurant?"

"Back door—no, Barlow just fell. There's ice on the—hey, put me down and we'll meet at my apartment."

He frowned down at her. "You want me to sneak around?"

"Well, yes. Why not?"

"We're getting married."

"I don't think so."

"Well, you're wrong." With that, he pushed open the door and carried her through the counter area to the dining room.

"They're getting married," she heard Heather tell a group of ranchers who had just come in for lunch. "We have to close up early."

Daisy hid her face against the warm sheepskin lining of Will's unzipped jacket. Tomorrow she would tell people she'd fainted and had to be carried out. She would explain that the "married" remark was Heather's idea of wit.

Will didn't kiss her until they reached her bedroom. He paused in front of the bed. "Sex first and talk later, or talk now and then sex?"

She had no willpower where he was concerned. "Sex first." Then she'd kick him out until she had time to think.

"Hmm," was all he said before he sat down on the bed with Daisy still tucked against him. "You're easy. It must be a trick."

"No trick." She wished he'd move his hand just a little higher.

"Don't try distracting me," he growled. "I have stuff to say."

"Like what?" Daisy began unbuttoning his shirt. This would be the absolute last time she would do this, she told herself. "I heard you were selling the ranch and leaving town."

"Hell, don't people have anything else to talk about?"

"I guess not." She parted his shirt but was faced with a white T-shirt. "You keep giving them so much to say."

"Stop that." He cupped her hands in one of his. "Before you say you'll marry me you'd better know what's going on."

Daisy raised her head and looked into that very handsome face. "All right."

"Spring's staying with me, so you'd have to adopt her with me."

She didn't dare believe that Spring would be—could be—hers after all. "And what about Sarah?"

"Is going back to college. She knows she's not old enough to raise a child and I think she's learned a lot in the past couple of years." He sighed. "At least I hope so. My grandfather pretty much drove her out of the house—he started knocking her around after

Epilogue

IF HE HADN'T awoken to feel his wife's warm breasts against his arm, he would never have heard the knock on the front door. He wasn't sure he heard anything at first, but the bedroom windows were open, letting a spring breeze caress the lace curtains and early-morning birds sing to the dawn.

Will eased out of the bed, then tucked the quilt around his wife's shoulders. The baby was due any day and lately Daisy had been pretty tired. He'd stopped spending time out at the ranch, though one of these days he and Daisy figured they'd build a place out there, within a few miles from the Pierce place.

The little knock came again, so Will pulled on his jeans and hurried down the stairs as quietly as he could. He opened the front door, but all he heard was a soft giggle. Will saw Maude Anderson waving from across the street, so he waved back. Then, on the step he saw a tiny basket filled with construction-paper flowers.

"It's a May basket, Daddy," a little voice said. Will turned around to see Spring peeking out at him from behind a rocking chair, Bozeman wagging his tail beside her. "Happy May Day."

"Hey, sweetheart," he said, kneeling down and holding out his arms for a hug. "It's very pretty."

"Is Mommy up?"

"Not yet."

Spring's blue eyes clouded over. "I made daisies. Like her."

Sure enough, when Will turned to pick up the basket he realized that the sticky, glue-spotted flowers looked something like daisies, though he wasn't exactly sure. "Then let's go take them to her."

He scooped her up into his arms and carried her upstairs, then tiptoed into the bedroom and let his daughter place the basket on the pillow beside Daisy.

"Mommy's happy," the little girl whispered.

"Of course she is," Will said, noting his wife's peaceful expression. "I think she's dreaming of Spring."

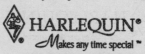